Meadows of Gold

C. L. Kraemer

Chapter One

A gentle breeze sighed, undulating the meadow grass lazily and whispering past the forlorn figure slumped on the tree trunk, hands clasped tightly in his lap. Thomas, a forest leprechaun, released a long melancholy breath between his cracked, dry lips. A single plump tear meandered down his stubbled cheek.

The sun sent bright shafts of light through the pine boughs and around the wooden pedestal upon which the morose figure resided. Ignoring the dancing beams, the leprechaun pulled a shuddered breath into his lungs and stared at a spot in front of the stump where a crumpled daisy chain necklace lay withering in the warmth of the afternoon. Another plump tear snaked down his unshaven face.

In the distance, a lone figure scuffed up the lane, which crossed in front of the tree stump. Thomas paid no heed to the approaching form, pulling a thin silver flask from inside his rumpled vest. He blindly opened the lid, placed the opened top to his lips and pulled a deep draught from the container. Refitting the cap to the top, he slipped the silver spirit holder back into his vest. His next shuddered breath was interrupted with a hiccup.

The figure on the road drew closer. Thomas raised his head and squinted his eyes. Was she coming back? He hiccupped and straightened up. Maybe she had been teasing him when she ran away and now she realized how much he cared for her. His eyes brightened and a smile began to touch his lips.

The figure came around the bend and toward him. The last he'd seen her, she was wearing a diaphanous, thin dress. Had she changed? The form nearing him was clad in leather breeches, a braided leather tunic, and knee-high, soft leather boots. A sword blade strapped to the figure's back flashed in the sunlight. Was Cary so angry she meant to cut him in little pieces?

His heart began to pound in his chest and inside his mouth his tongue stuck to the roof.

The figure stopped two lengths from him and raised a hand to shade its eyes from the brightness of the day.

Thomas realized he was shaking. This was it…his life was over. He hung his head.

"Thomas?"

The voice was familiar but it didn't sound like Cary. If it wasn't her…

~ * ~

"Thomas! What are you doing?" Tiamoon, a warrior gnome of the valley clan, stood with her feet planted shoulder width apart in her full leather armor on the roadway to her home. She'd just reconnoitered the meadow area for evidence of the marauding night elves. The local hill clan had been raiding the gnome settlements and wreaking havoc on the inhabitants. The gnome community was rallying together to protect their families against further damage.

Thomas narrowed his eyes and looked through his veil of tears.

"Oh, Tia (hic) moon, itsch you."

Tia rolled her eyes heavenward and leaned toward the wobbling leprechaun, wrinkling her nose in disgust at the sour smell of alcohol surrounding the disheveled lump occupying the tree stump.

"Thomas? How long have you been sitting here?"

"Dunno. What day is it?"

"Tuesday."

"Really?" Thomas lifted rheumy eyes to meet Tiamoon's clear blue ones.

"Yes, really. So how long have you been here, Thomas?"

"Uhm, (hic) since Saturday."

"Saturday!"

Tiamoon stepped to the stump, in the process crushing the daisy chain necklace. She reached out to grab the leprechaun as he dissolved in tears.

"You (hic)… you stepped on (hic) the necklace. (hic) Just like she (hic) stepped on my heart."

"Good heavens, Thomas, pull yourself together. She who?"

She wrestled the drunken leprechaun to his unsteady feet. His weight surprised her. He was sturdy and muscular beneath the rumpled clothing.

"Cary, the love of my life."

"Heavens be cursed. Thomas…"

"Wha-a-a?" He turned red-rimmed, green orbs her direction.

"You fall in love with every female who crosses your path."

"Do *not*!"

"Really? Okay let me guess…she flirted with you and teased you until she got you out here at the edge of the meadow where you promised to tell her where your secret stash of gold was hidden if she'd kiss you and be your mate."

His eyes ricocheted in the sockets, making Tiamoon's head hurt.

"You were (hic) sshpying on ussh."

Tia got her shoulder under his armpit and hoisted him up. She wrinkled her nose at the stale body odor emanating from his clothing.

"No, Thomas. It's a pattern everyone in the woods knows. Come on. You need a bath, some food and sleep."

"But what if (hic) she comesh back?"

"Thomas? I can guarantee that won't happen today. Come on."

She dragged him along the road. His head was slumped on his chest and his leather shoes were dragging, toes down, in the soft dirt of the two-lane thoroughfare. After a mile of struggling with the leprechaun, she turned down a single file path winding through the trees. Thomas had hiccupped in Tia's ear through the entire journey, his head lolling from side to side.

She'd reached the end of the path as well as the end of her patience. When the path stopped abruptly at the river's edge, so did Tia. She allowed the momentum of her pace to transfer to the inert leprechaun.

The moment the figure hit the icy water, he screamed.

"You're killing me! Gods in Heaven! You're trying to kill me!"

"For crying out loud, Thomas. Just dunk your head under the water and quit yelling. Maybe if you bathed more often, you wouldn't chase away the ladies."

The figure floundered in the icy stream.

"I can't swim! Tia! I'm drowning!"

"Thomas?"

"Help! I'm drowning!"

"THOMAS!"

The roar echoed through the woods.

"Put your feet down!"

Blustering until his face was crimson, the drunken man splashed furiously. His head went beneath the water and he rose up sputtering, unconsciously standing on the stream's bottom. He quit flailing his arms.

"Oh."

"Yeah, oh." Tia drew her sword and pointed it his direction. "Now get yourself and your clothing sopping wet. If you even think of getting on the bank without attempting to wash off some of that stench, I'll split you from gullet to gizzard."

He glared at the gnome warrior.

"Fine."

She stood pointing her sharpened blade at him until he and his clothing were sufficiently soaked.

"Now, let's go. My mom will have some stew to put into your stomach."

"But I don't wa..."

Thomas stopped his whine at the glare he was receiving from Tia.

"Lead the way."

Chapter Two

Cary stretched her arms above her head as she yawned. Her moss bed lay in a sunspot inside her temporary oak tree home and she took every opportunity available to steal a nap. Today was no exception. She'd had a run-in with the leprechaun Thomas. He'd gotten sloppy drunk and proposed a union between the two and had the nerve to act surprised when she'd turned him down.

Had he been so drunk as to think his offer of gold could sway her?

"Fool. I have something worth more than his pitiful pot of gold."

She splashed water on her face from the acorn bowl nitched in the cradle of the root of her tree. She wiped her face and hands with an oak leaf. Staring out a gap that served as a window, she noted the rippling heat waves rising to the cloudless sky from the swaying meadow grass. The wind blew hot across her face and she turned from the opening to nibble on some bread. It had been a strange fortnight. Cary still wasn't sure *exactly* what had occurred. She and Conn had been scheming, no, make that planning to undo the wedding of Casey and Kelly and were in right good position to see that happen when, whoosh! they were spirited away along with that pompous human, Florence to--here, wherever here was.

The rustlings across the room set aside Cary's concentration and alerted her to the fact Conn was beginning to move about from his nap.

"Have we food?"

Cary looked at her rumpled roommate. "Always thinking with your stomach, aren't you? If the bread I secured is not enough for your fine palette, then get out and find suitable food."

"Why do I have to be the one to supply the meals?"

Cary fisted her tiny hands to her hips and cast a deadly glare at

Conn.

"Because of all the talents in this world, you're gifted at putting food on the table."

He slogged his way to the sink and splashed water on his face. He sucked in a surprised breath.

"That's cold!"

"Might be because the water flows directly from the stream?"

Conn wiped his face and hands and headed for the makeshift door.

"I'm out to find food and trace the whereabouts of Florence. As we have lived in this… place for a fortnight, my senses tell me he might be in need of my services. Left alone to his own devices, he fares poorly.

"I'll return then we can sit down and make plans to locate Casey and Kelly. They've been having enough time to learn to dislike each other by now. Our plans will be easy enough to initiate. This time next week, all will be as it should."

"Are you daft?" Cary fluttered to land lightly on her feet in front of Conn.

"Beg pardon?" A scowl covered his face.

"We're not in the green isles, you fool. We're of a different time and different place. I know not exactly and will be out myself to see if I can steal the knowledge from one of the locals. When I have this information, we'll talk about what plans to make. Not before. You go and hunt for Florence, but don't return reeking of wine and foolishness." Cary stamped her foot and turned her back to Conn.

His face reddened and he yanked open the piece of wood they'd been using as a door. He let the bark drop on the ground and flew from the tree.

He buzzed close to the earth, taking in the smells of this new place. There was much greenery here and the trees grew tall and lush. He had to admit to himself Cary was right. This was not the Ireland he knew. What he could smell of the earth was dark, fertile ground. His ears caught the sound of a very angry, very large horde of bees. He shifted his direction and came upon a scene foreign to his eyes. Strangely dressed humans held shiny steel weapons. They seemed to be attacking the forest with a tree-eating monster that buzzed very loudly while eating its way through the wooded area.

Conn was frightened and shot away from the scene. Though certain he could not be seen, he wished not to take any chances. He heard a loud rattling sound and the grinding of metal-to-metal coming very close to him. Darting to hide behind a large evergreen, he peeked at the aberration that nearly crushed him.

It was very large and black. The wheels upon the black wagon had a foreign substance all around them. This padding substance was why the large cart approached him in relative silence. There did not seem to be any horses at the front pulling but the metallic cart moved forward with a deafening high pitched grinding of metal. The wagon stirred up the dust and dirt on the trail. Conn felt a tickle in his nose and, before he could think, he sneezed loudly.

"Ach! I can't be giving away my location. Who knows what monsters lie in wait in this forest? I need to find Florence. I have seen more abominations today than I care to ponder. The explanations must surely be simple."

Conn lifted his wings and tentatively flew toward the direction where the sun slid behind the hills. He sensed Florence. With each wing beat, his sensation of his ward grew stronger. He would find his charge and answers would be forthcoming. Until that time, he was charged with being vigilant and wary. Despite Cary's warning, Conn knew he was going to need some mead to settle his nerves.

"She can threaten all she wants, but until she's been as close to the mouth of this monster as I, she can't know the terror. Only mead can soothe this kind of fear."

Having justified his visit to the pub, Conn let a smile touch his lips. Finding Florence was important but not as important as Conn settling his nerves. He couldn't be expected to pump information from his charge and find food without a bit of the mead, could he?

Of course not. He began to whistle a lively reel as he flew toward town. This would turn out to be a positive day after all.

~ * ~

Cary was irritated at Conn. It really was his fault they were in this mess. If he'd been watching Kelly as he was supposed to instead of dashing about the fight egging the boys on, they'd still be back home in familiar surroundings instead of this place. She had no name for this land. All she knew was everything recognizable had disappeared. She needed to find a place where she could get the information without giving away her ignorance. Cary hovered just above the grass line. She sensed other beings close by and headed their direction. As the human voices grew louder, she slowed her flying, finally touching down near a whitewashed building sporting a porch out front. Silently, she climbed up the boxes on the front to look into the window. Her eyes beheld a business selling assorted items. She could hear a bell ring and decided to investigate.

She skittered inside the opened door and sidled up to the wooden counter. Peeking around the side, she noted items in jars on shelves behind the front counter. A human with a white apron stood behind the divider and helped other humans by retrieving merchandise from the containers on the shelves. He would then go to a large metal box, pushed some metal things jutting out from the box and stand back while a portion on the bottom of the box jumped out at him. It was the box which made the bell sound. Cary had flown up to the counter to investigate the box when her skin dimpled in chill bumps. *Someone is watching me!*

She raised her eyes to look directly into the cool, blue orbs of a female night elf. Cary panicked. Night elves! She had not encountered a night elf in years. Now, in this place where she knew nothing, she was going to have to keep her guard up against night elves?

Before Cary could react, Gitty Saun casually leaned over and snatched the faery from her hiding place and placed the tiny being in her leather carryall.

"Curses on your father!" the little fae screamed to the darkened leather prison walls.

Well, now she'd done it. She was no smarter for her travel and her current state of freedom was in question. Cary dropped her chin to her hand as she sat on something metallic and uncomfortable. The jouncing of the bag as this creature walked was making her nauseous. If she had been but a moment quicker…

She twittered then chuckled and finally allowed herself the luxury of laughing out loud. She had to give credit to this giant--were she able she would have made the same move. She could only hope the appetizer for tonight's dinner was not being carried in this leather prison.

Chapter Three

Florence sat in his room squinting out the window. He had indeed indulged himself a bit too much last evening. The light in his eyes pierced through his head causing the muscles of his neck to spasm in pain. If he were just to have a bit of the powder the witch woman in his village kept on hand, he might survive this day.

A tap upon his door sent him to moaning.

"What would you ask of me now?" Florence pushed the heels of his palms against his eyes.

"Mr. Florence? It's Dorinda. May I come in?"

His head ached and he tried his best to recall a Dorinda. When the door opened a crack and the smell of fresh soap assailed his nose, his brain kicked into gear.

Ah, yes; the slender serving wench from the tavern.

"Please, my lady. Do enter my chamber."

The door hinges complained with a high-pitched squeal, setting his ears to twitching and his head to pounding.

"Ah, lass. Could you be but a wee bit quieter?"

"So sorry, Mr. Florence. I thought you might be...hungover a bit from last night. I brought some aspirin to help relieve the pain. If you swallow them with this glass of water, it should help take away some of the pain in about twenty minutes."

Dorinda placed two aspirin on the table next to the glass of water she'd brought.

Florence lifted bloodshot eyes to the night table then to his uninvited guest.

"What's this poison you place before me? A draft to kill?"

Dorinda's face drained of color, her eyes widening in horror.

"Oh, no, Mr. Florence! This is medicine to relieve the pain. If you don't want to take it, I'll take the pills away."

Florence looked at the tiny white spots on the table stained with brown rings and burn spots.

"This not be poison?"

Dorinda vigorously shook her head.

"Medicine to take this evil from my head in less than the peal of one bell?"

She hesitantly nodded.

"Then I shall ingest this...medicine and wait to see if you skirt the truth. But know this, woman, should I expire from your ministrations I shall curse you and all the kinsmen of your clan."

He put the pill into his mouth and started to chew.

"NO!"

Florence squinted his eyes and hunched his shoulders against the reverberation of the shout in his head.

"Swallow the pills whole and wash them down with the water."

Bitterness exploded in his mouth, and he sensed he was close to losing the contents of his stomach. He lifted the glass and washed down the remainder of the pills. A hint of sweetness remained on his tongue as he swallowed to quell the bile rising up his throat.

Dorinda took the glass from his hand.

"When your headache is gone, come to the kitchen and I'll make you breakfast."

A slight nod of his head sent her out of the room. Florence lay back on the soft bed and closed his eyes. His head spun from the events of the last fortnight. The strange clothing on his body had appeared after he had first stumbled into the inn and had been subjected to the jeering of the patrons. The slender serving wench had taken pity on him and steered him to this room he occupied. Somewhere she had secured the local dress of the area so he would not appear out of place. But he *was* out of place and it was up to him to determine his whereabouts so he could return to his life in the emerald land of his birth.

He was respected in his home village. People knew his father was a wealthy man and they catered to his wishes. Somehow the knowledge had not traveled to this village. He would have to right the situation.

Florence's eyes drooped then closed as the aspirin began to work. Within fifteen minutes, he was snoring, the headache temporarily forgotten.

~ * ~

Cary was close to losing the battle with her stomach when the swaying stopped and her leather prison was unceremoniously thumped on to a solid, unmoving surface. As she stood up and tried to get her legs under her, the top of the bag was wrenched open, blasting a glaring light directly on the little fae causing her to throw her hand over her eyes.

"Well, well, well. What do we have here?"

A large, porcelain colored extremity snatched the wee folk by her waist and pulled her into the light of the room.

Cary blinked furiously, trying to adjust her eyes to the surroundings. The abode was as large as any castle she'd seen but not hewn together with any stone she recognized.

A magnificent fireplace stood guard at an end wall but no logs crackled a warm welcome. The furnishings scattered about the room were bulky, imposing and cold, making the little fae shiver.

The large fingers wrapped around the fae exuded warmth. Cary tried to wiggle herself free to no avail.

"I don't think even you have the strength to escape my grip, but you're welcome to try."

Cary turned and cast a wary look in the direction of the speaker.

"How is it you can see me?" She tilted her head to one side considering the tall, pale blonde with fair complexion.

"Because, wee one, I'm not a human."

Cary raised a brow, the hint of a smile touching her mouth. "No?"

Gitty pulled up one side of her lip and snarled. "No! I'd rather have my heart ripped out and fed to me than be part of the human race." She held her chin high. "*I* am a night elf. We are far more clever, smarter, better looking and live considerably longer than those human curs. *And* we are able to see magical creatures of the forest."

Cary pursed her lips together. She crossed her arms and considered this creature that had hold of her.

"So you can see the fae?"

"Yes, and because I can see the fae of the woods, I know you're a newcomer to this area. Who are you and where did you come from?"

Cary stared into the icy blue eyes of this night elf. No warmth radiated from their depths. In fact, she could see nothing resembling compassion in the elf's eyes no matter how hard she looked. She pulled up as straight as she could, unfolding her arms and adjusting her skirt.

"I am Cary of Innisboffin and I have absolutely no idea where *here* is. Maybe you could be so kind as to tell me where I am?"

Gitty chuckled. "Why so you can enchant me and leave? I don't think so. I think, for the time being, you'll be a guest in my home. When I feel I can trust you, I'll let you go, but not until then. So, wee one...back in the bag."

"NO!" Cary squirmed and pushed at the extremity clutching her body so tightly. "I hate the dark and that leather thing makes me sick. Please don't!" She sobbed and struggled, using all her strength. But alas, she was dumped unceremoniously into the pouch and the top was tightened closed.

"Now, what?"

Hiccupping and sobbing, Cary covered her face. Because of that darn Florence and his curiosity, she and Conn were who knows where. The clothing, language and homes she'd seen so far indicated this was not her beautiful Ireland. But if this was not Ireland, then where in all the world could she have landed?

It was a question whose answer would have to wait. Cary's eyelids traveled to her cheeks and before long the gentle snoring of a tiny faerie emanated from the leather pouch.

~ * ~

Florence woke to the sun streaming in his room. He reached up and touched his head, noting there was no pain remaining. Gingerly, he swung his legs to the floor and sat on the edge of the bed.

"The little white dots the wench gave me worked. My pain has passed and I'm starved. Think I'll find my way to the kitchen for a meal."

After a brief stop at the facilities, Florence entered the kitchen, his nose taking in the pungent smells.

"Ah, lass. what do you have for me this beautiful morn?"

Dorinda turned and graced him with a shy smile. "Morning, again, Mr. Florence. How does pork, potatoes and scrambled eggs sound to you?"

"Like a bit of heaven." *And home.*

"Looks as though the aspirin worked for you."

"Indeed it did, lass. I feel ready to take on the world." Florence noted the sudden sadness in the innkeeper's eyes. "What is it? Has something I said offended you?"

"No, sir. Just your comment about taking on the world leaves me no choice but to let you know of the consequences of your actions last night. You might want to take a seat."

Florence swallowed and pulled out the chair at the kitchen table. He plopped down.

Dorinda fussed around the stove shoveling eggs, bacon and fried potatoes on the platter. She placed the food in front of her boarder who grabbed his fork and dug into the meal. She added a plate of toast on the table within arm's reach.

She poured two cups of coffee, placing one in front of Florence. He grabbed the cup and started to gulp the contents.

"I wouldn't..."

"Owww! That's hot!"

Sitting at the chair opposite, Dorinda cradled her own cup between her hands. "As I was about to tell you, it's very hot. You might want to let it cool for a bit."

Florence touched his fingers to his burnt lip. "Right. Now what were you going to tell me about last night?"

Dorinda gazed into the dark contents inside her mug. She took a small sip then blew out a shuddered breath.

Florence grabbed a piece of toast and mopped up the remaining bits of food from the plate. When he finished the toast, he brushed his hands over the plate, shoved the soiled platter to the center of the table and leaned back to enjoy his coffee.

"Well?"

"Well, Mr. Florence, you insulted one of the new landowners in the valley who you challenged to a duel."

Florence's mouth dropped open. "I what?"

Dorinda squirmed in the chair. "You challenged him to a duel."

Pulling up, he placed the mug of coffee on the table and cleared his throat.

"How...how did that happen?"

"Best as I can tell, you called his girlfriend a saucy trollop and he took offense."

Florence lowered his head to his hands. "I take it he feels the need to defend her honor?"

"Yep. And as drunk as you were, you challenged him to a duel with swords."

Florence groaned. "I'm much better with a pistol."

"Too late. The duel is set for this evening at the edge of the meadow. If you don't show, he'll hunt you down and 'dispatch you'."

I've done it now. Not only do I have no idea where I might be but I've riled up the villagers. Florence huffed out a breath. "Tis done now. Have you a blade with which I might practice?"

Dorinda lifted a brow. She rose from the table and reached beside the icebox, retrieving a worn sweeper, its bristles splayed and bent.

"No, Mr. Florence. But I do have a broom. Best I can do on such short notice."

Florence took the proffered weapon, glancing up and down the shaft.

"Will have to do. Thank you, Miss Dorinda. Should anyone seek me, I'll be in the yard… practicing. Please call me in time to clean up before I leave for the inn."

Dorinda hid a smirk. "As you wish, Mr. Florence." *He's gonna get himself killed.*

~ * ~

Conn slipped past a farmer in bib overalls as he opened the door to the inn. The fae winged his way to a corner of the pub and watched the assorted villagers enter and leave. His thirst was increasing with the passing of each human. This place didn't have a designated corner as they did back in his land where the humans understood fae still existed in the land. How was he to slake his thirst if no one offered him mead? His mood darkened until a movement from the corner of his eye caught his attention.

Sitting with his back to the wall, a tall, elegant man ordered himself a glass of mead with a second smaller container set to the side. He carefully moved his long, blonde locks behind his shoulder and looked directly at Conn.

The fae held his breath and froze in his position.

"I can see you, little brother. Come sit with me. Surely, you thirst?"

Conn's heart thundered in his chest. He was certain the man had been speaking to another.

"Come. I *can* see you, wee one. I know you must have a great thirst. Join me and quench the fire in your mouth." The hint of a smile touched the blue-eyed man's lips.

Conn was sorely tempted. This stranger had a familiarity about him that made Conn cautious. The long blond hair, blue eyes and ability to see the fae? He shuddered. A night elf; what were night elves doing in this faraway place?

I'm so thirsty but if this elf captures me...oh, what the heck. What more do I have to lose except my thirst? Conn winged his way to the table and landed just out of reach of the elf.

"Greetings, kind sir."

The elf slid the small glass toward the fae.

"And to you, sir."

"Call me Morgan."

"And I'm Conn." The little fae eyed the elf warily. "Can you be trusted, Morgan?"

The corners of Morgan's lips curled in delight.

"I sincerely hope not."

Conn blinked his eyes, furrowing his brow then threw his head back and laughed.

"Ah, good. A man after my own heart. I think we shall get along."

Morgan dipped his head and grabbed his glass.

"You speak the truth, Conn. To a new...partnership."

Conn pushed his glass toward the elf, furiously using his wings to move the large container.

"To a new partnership." He then stuck his head in the glass and pulled a deep draught from the amber liquid.

"Ptah! This is milk for children!"

"You speak the truth but it is the best these villagers can produce. It's better than water."

"Well spoken."

The unlikely twosome drank quietly. When the liquid dropped so far down the glass the fae was unable to get to it, Morgan signaled to the barmaid to bring a straw.

"What brings you to this inn, Conn?"

Conn was certain Florence had frequented this place but was still a bit leery of the night elf.

"I felt a need to drown my thirst and observe the humans of this village. Has there been any excitement lately?"

Morgan downed his drink and signaled for another. "Yes, there has. Some blighter showed up a fortnight ago and started horning in on my territory, if you know what I mean?"

Conn took a pull from his straw, eliminating the need to answer.

"Anyway, he comes prancing through the door last night like some nancy-boy and sidles up to my companion for the evening. After several glasses of whiskey, he made a rude comment about her character when she rebuffed his advances."

Good heavens, Florence. Not in town for a moon and you've poisoned the water. Maybe you don't need my help.

"What happened?" Conn balanced himself on the rim of the glass.

"I demanded he apologize to the lady and myself. He laughed, issued more inappropriate suggestions regarding my lady friend then challenged me to a duel."

Conn slipped from the rim and saved himself from falling in the mead by quickly winging his way to the tabletop.

"Does your sheriff *allow* dueling? In my village, the sheriff would lock everyone up should he have knowledge of such a happening."

"I'm above these quaint humans laws. I live by my own rules."

The elfkind's wrinkled nose and down turned lips showed his disgust for the local constabulary.

Conn gulped. He had to ask the question burning in his brain.

"Wha-what weapon did he choose?"

Morgan allowed a big smile to lighten his face.

"Fool chose blades."

Conn started coughing.

"Are you alright, friend?"

The fae held up one hand while the other clutched his stomach. He nodded then lowered his head to his knees in an attempt to catch his breath. Once he had his composure back, he pulled upright and continued.

"Can I assume you're talented with the blade?"

Morgan's smile widened. "If I say so myself, I'm very adept with steel."

Oh, you've done it now, Florence.

Conn moved to his perch on the glass' edge.

"So, what would this nancy-boy's name be, Morgan?" He pulled in a mouthful of beer and quickly swallowed.

"I've no idea. What does it matter?"

"The name will be important for placing on the headstone."

"Ah, my little friend, you do have a point. Let me see..." Morgan tapped his finger on his chin. "I believe it was Terrance. No, more along the lines of Lawrence to the best of my recollection. I wasn't really interested in his name; just his apology to my lady friend."

"As well you should have been. If interlopers are allowed to insult your companions, they'll have no compunction about insulting you. You can't have that in your village."

"Thank you, Conn. It's good to see someone who understands my position. I'm afraid my sister isn't as comprehending of a gentleman's duties."

Conn looked at the elf lounging elegantly in the opposite chair. He'd just mentioned a sister so that meant there were at least two of these night elves in the vicinity. He wondered how many were in their clan.

"Tell me, Morgan. When is this duel to occur?"

"This afternoon at the set of the sun."

"Shouldn't you be practicing?"

"His defeat can be accomplished with one hand held behind my back."

"Maybe I'll stick around and observe."

Morgan signaled the barmaid. "I'm feeling a mite peckish. Would you care for dinner?"

"Love some."

Conn smiled. His day had morphed from dismal to delightful in the span of one glass of beer. He and Cary may have been stranded here because of Florence but Conn was going to make the very best of it. If Florence had to be sacrificed in the process, well, such were the consequences.

The barmaid brought soup in a bowl for Morgan and, at Morgan's request, a small cupful for *the wee ones* he'd told the barmaid with a wink.

She shook her head and rolled her eyes but complied with his request, as he was known to be a big tipper.

Conn tucked into the soup. *I could get used to this. Wonder where Cary is?*

The thought flitted in and out of his mind. He was too busy eating and drinking to give it any real consideration. Things would turn out as they were destined. They always did.

Chapter Four

Tiamoon had settled Thomas at the family table after coaxing him to change into dry clothing she'd located in her brother's room.

"Don't even think of moving." She narrowed her eyes at the weaving leprechaun.

Thomas picked at the sleeve of the shirt. "This isn't mine. Where's my clothing?"

Tia unbelted her sword and placed it inside a small closet beneath the stairs of the cottage.

"Your clothes are out on the line drying. Maybe some fresh air will help rid them of the stench."

She went in search of her mother. In the back of the small building, divided into equally marked plots, lay the pride and joy of Tiamoon's mother, Skye--her garden. From the cool, damp days of spring through summer's heat, Skye charmed the earth into producing bushels of food. It was in this haven Tiamoon located her.

"Hello, mum."

"Hello, Tia. Can you hand me the trowel near your feet?"

Tia picked up the small spade and carried it to her mother.

"I've brought home Thomas, the leprechaun from the meadow clan. I was hoping you might have some of your potato soup left."

"There's some on the stove. Why did you bring him here?"

"He's a mess. He's been drinking for who knows how long and was visible to any that chose to look. He'd have given us away to the humans."

Skye rose from her knees to face her youngest child. "Daughter, you have to stop bringing home strays." Patting Tia on the shoulder as she passed, she moved in the direction of the cottage. "I'll warm the stew but you have to make the toast."

Tia surveyed the bounty of fresh food growing in the plot. Every year she watched her mom create life from the earth and it still amazed her. She hadn't the patience. Clashing swords was more her style.

Skye had stoked the fire and was stirring the warming soup when Tia strode into the room. On the small table next to the drain board sat the wire toaster and a couple slices of bread. Tia popped a slice into the wire and with a dishtowel opened the heated handle of the cast iron wood stove. Mere minutes provided the needed heat to brown the bread. Smearing the toast with fresh churned butter, she placed it on a small plate and, with a full bowl of heated soup in her other hand, carried the food to the dining table and the sleeping leprechaun.

Tia placed the food far enough away from Thomas as to be safe, then walked to his chair and shook him awake.

"Get up, you fool. My mother has worked hard to provide food for your mangy self. Least you can do is eat it."

Wiping away the drool from his lips, he leaned back and inhaled deeply.

"Smells to be a good potato soup--and toast. I, uh, I think I might actually be hungry." His eyes opened wide and he grabbed for the dishes.

Tia slapped a hand on the table next to his watching him jump in reaction.

"Now that I've got your attention, listen up. You'll eat politely and not make a mess. You'll finish everything on these plates then you'll excuse yourself and wash up. After that, I'm putting you in my brother's room for the night. Tomorrow, you'll go home and stay away from the spirits until next week. Do I make myself clear?"

Thomas nodded, his attention riveted on the steaming bowl of soup.

Tia slid the bowl to him and retrieved a spoon from the sideboard.

She handed him the implement. "Politely."

Watching him devour the contents of the bowl, Tia wondered how he ever managed to take care of himself. Seemed someone in the meadow was always looking after him. *Might be how he planned it.* Tia looked hard at the leprechaun. *Nah, not clever enough.*

She walked to the front of the small cottage and stared out the window to the meadow. The name Thomas had uttered in his drunken stupor was new. She was familiar with most of the meadow, forest and mountain fae in this area and none bore this assignation of Cary. It rang of the old country. She would have to investigate this new visitor.

The loud buzz of snoring interrupted her thought and Tia turned to find Thomas asleep at the table. She bundled him from the chair and dragged him back to her brother's room. Securing him in the bed, she closed the door and went to sit in front of the cottage where she gazed at the scenery.

She couldn't quite put her finger on the uneasiness roiling about her. Her nerves tingled on the top of her skin and she jumped with the slightest provocation. A change was about to happen to her valley, Tia was sure. Just what that change was--she wouldn't even hazard a guess.

~ * ~

Cary moaned and rolled to her back. This was absurd. Why was she tiptoeing around this night elf? The wee folk had taught many of them the magic they used! She had more ability in her tiny finger than the cold hearted, stony-eyed giantess who held her captive had in her entire body. Mustering her courage, Cary stood and began to chant a spell her mother had taught her. Again and again, she chanted the lines, feeling the dormant power surge through her veins. Radiance began to glow around her and the leather container opened. Cary zipped through the mouth of the bag, coming face to face with the night elf.

"I wondered how long it would take before you employed your power." Gitty smirked and reached to grab the tiny fae.

Cary loop-de-looped away, winging herself a safe distance from the elf. "You'll not be holding me prisoner any longer."

Gitty swiped at the floating fae and missed again. A frown marred the porcelain face. "And what makes you think I can't?"

Cary flew straight at the elf and stopped directly in front of her.

"Because the width and breath of my magic surpasses anything you can imagine. I'll have no hesitation to use it to bring you to my size and pummel the life from you!"

Sparks flew from the wee one's fingertips as she pointed at Gitty.

The two stood staring at each other; Cary hovering in front of the elf and the night elf standing feet planted shoulder width apart, hands on hips, glaring.

The air crackled and popped. Wind whipped hair wildly around their heads. The clock on the fire's mantle ticked loudly, echoing in the silence of the room.

Then Cary giggled. Gitty raised her eyebrows and a smile hovered over her lips. The tiny fae clutched her sides as she broke into laughter, her shoulders shaking.

Gitty snickered and soon was laughing as well.

The wee one drifted to the shoulder of the night elf.

"I must say, Madam Night Elf, you seem to be a soul after my own heart. What say we join forces? I can use a partner in this new place who has knowledge and position."

Gitty chuckled. "You've proven yourself bold, Cary. I believe you have the flint of a steel blade backed by the powers of a great mage. Your convenient size would help me in my pursuits, too. We have the makings of a perfect partnership.

"Shall we call it done?"

The wee fae flit off Gitty's shoulder and pirouetted in front of her.

"Done!"

Chapter Five

Florence pulled the handkerchief from his back pocket and swiped at his forehead. He couldn't remember the last time he'd sweat this much. Tucking the soaked cloth in his pocket, he picked up his broom and began the parry-lunge-withdraw routine his father had taught him as a boy.

My only hope is the lessons father tried to impart to me will come back automatically.

"Mr. Florence? Mr. Florence?"

Dorinda carried a glass of sparkling water to the red-faced warrior. She handed the cooling liquid to him and watched as he gulped the contents.

"I think you should come inside and have dinner."

"I'm not really hungry."

"It will help to bolster your strength and spirit. You might also consider a shower before you leave. I've washed your clothing and shined your boots. You'll look very dashing in your outfit."

Florence stopped and turned to look at Dorinda. Her blue eyes gave no hint of guile.

"Sounds a good idea to me. I'll shower before dinner, if you don't mind."

"Not at all." *Whew. I'm glad he suggested it first.*

She led the way to the kitchen.

Florence continued to the bathing room and found his clothing carefully laid out. He admired the high gloss of his riding boots and noted his shirt had never been so spotless. It appeared nearly new. He held the trousers to his nose and pulled in the scent of fresh air. His hand lightly caressed the sharp crease, which had been ironed into the fabric. He'd wash himself especially well using some of the sweet smelling soap in the bathing room then smooth his hair with the slicker Dorinda had shown him how to use.

He strolled into the dining room, his nose seduced by the delicious smells coming from the kitchen.

"Have a seat at the table."

Florence set in the chair where a plate and silverware had been placed.

Dorinda brought in a plate of crisp, golden fried chicken. She set it on the towel and slapped at Florence's extended hand.

"Not until all the food has been brought out."

He licked his lips. His stomach complained loudly but he knew not to push his luck.

Dorinda finished placing mashed potatoes, homemade gravy, baked biscuits, home grown corn and fresh butter and honey on the table.

"Now we say grace."

The two bowed their heads and Dorinda offered the blessing.

"Lord, please bless this food and those who eat it. Watch over Mr. Florence tonight so he returns safely to our house. Amen."

"Amen."

Florence looked at Dorinda and raised his eyebrows.

She smiled shyly. "Yes, Mr. Florence, you may start." *Eat hearty, man. This may be your last meal.*

~ * ~

The buzz around the meadow increased all through the day.

Tiamoon snagged Cheney, head of the wood clan of gnomes, as he headed toward his forest home and asked about all the excitement.

"Haven't you heard?"

"Would I have asked if I had heard, Cheney?" Tia frowned and crossed her arms.

"Uh, right. We've had visitors arrive in the last two weeks who seem discontent with the peace of our valley."

"What are you talking about?"

"A human arrived and was accompanied by a couple of fae I've not seen before." Cheney nodded his head at the fact.

"You wouldn't happen to have the name of the fae, would you?" Tia dropped her arms to her sides.

He furrowed his brow and narrowed his eyes. "To the best of my recollection, the she-fae is called Mary. No, that's not it. Derry, no, humph." His eyes rolled to the sky as he thought. "Cary! That's it. She's Cary and he's Conn. The human they accompanied has some fancy girly name like Flossie, or Francis. Something like that."

So this was the name of the fae Thomas the Leprechaun muttered in his drunken stupor.

"What has all the valley folk wagging their tongues so furiously?"

"The human male challenged Morgan to a duel...with swords." Cheney's grin covered his face.

"Is the man out of his mind?!" Tia began to pace. "He'll be skewered. We can't have these humans and night elves dueling in our valley. If the human is killed, the human authorities will come out here and trample our homes in their zeal to find the culprit."

"Hmm. Hadn't thought of that."

"Apparently nobody has. When and where is this to happen?"

"Tonight at the meadow's edge. All the valley-kind will be there. Listen, I want to go home and eat before the duel. I'll see you there, Tia."

With a quick wave of his hand, Cheney disappeared into the greenery of the forest.

It was bad enough the night elves were raiding the homes of the faerie and gnome clans. With teamwork and dedication, the gnomes, faeries, wood nymphs and other small folk of the valley might be able to protect their homes and hold back the scourge of the elves. If humans got involved in the mix, the valley folk would surely lose.

Tia shuddered at the thought. With someone else responsible for patrolling the meadows and forests tonight, she'd planned a quiet evening at home. Taking care of Thomas had drained her energy. However, her quiet evening would have to wait.

Anytime the night elves were involved in a fracas, nothing good happened from outcome. Tiamoon needed to witness this event and plan accordingly.

~ * ~

Morgan pulled the brush through his white hair one last time, settling the locks behind his shoulders.

"Looking magnificent." He smiled at the reflection in the mirror.

"My lord, brother. You're worse than any human woman I've met. I take it you have a heated rendezvous tonight?"

Morgan slowly turned to face his sister. "I have a meeting but not with one of the local women." A smile touched one corner of his mouth accenting the dimple in his cheek.

"I've been challenged to a duel."

Gitty had sprawled across the white divan. Her eyes grew in astonishment."You? Dueling? Please. Whatever brought this on?"

"There's a cretin of a human being who showed up a couple weeks ago and tried to sweet talk his way into my territory. Last evening was the final straw. He insulted my lady friend and I demanded an apology.

"He's the one who challenged me to a duel. He just made the mistake of choosing swords."

Gitty sat up and considered her brother. "Well, if nothing else, I can give you the edge on swords. Next to me, you're the best swordsman in the clan."

Morgan rolled his eyes. "I can outfight you any day, sister. Once I've finished this interloper, we can set a time and date to meet and prove who's best."

Gitty propped her feet on the table in front of the divan.

"No thanks, little brother. I've better things to do with my time than beat you soundly at a sword fight."

Morgan huffed out an impatient breath. "I haven't time for this. I'll be at the meadow's edge at twilight should you wish to witness my victory."

He flipped his cape over one shoulder and pulled open the heavy wooden door, allowing it to close behind him.

Gitty turned to the small figure seated quietly on the back of the divan."Well, Cary, fancy a night on the town?"

The little fae's eyes lit up. "Yes!" She flew up and turned a somersault before landing on the night elf's shoulder.

"Lead the way, partner."

Chapter Six

Rays of rose-colored light extended warm fingers from the setting sun to the golden meadow in the valley. Surrounding mountain sentinels glowed a deep burgundy and purple, hiding their forests in indigo shadows.

Standing head and shoulders above the gathering crowd, a lone white-haired figure towered, replete with flowing cape and polished black boots. Securely tucked at the figure's side in a hand-tooled leather scabbard shone a finely honed sword engraved with the bearer's name and family crest. At his feet, a plain practice weapon reclined.

Morgan unconsciously brushed his hair behind his shoulders as he unbuttoned his cloak. With a flourish worthy of a film star, he whipped the cape from his shoulders and folded the plush material in one smooth motion. Sunlight flashed off the hardened steel blade and he placed his bundle on the cleanest log he could find.

Conn winged to the cape and took a seat. He winked at Morgan and wiggled his brows. There was nothing quite as exciting as a good fight. Rubbing his hands together, he giggled. If Morgan quickly dispatched his opponent, maybe they could go to the pub and have more mead before he went back to face Cary.

With carefully staged movements, Morgan drew his weapon from the scabbard, the quiet hissing of the blade against the leather lost in the growing murmur of the multitude.

Morgan was a patient man, but the cowardice of his opponent was becoming evident by the lack of his presence. Should the interloper fail to appear, he would win by default and not have to break a sweat. He felt confident this stranger was more bluff than action. More to his advantage. He would appear as the wounded party and fall back in the good graces of the ladies.

Just as Morgan decided to resheath his weapon, a ruckus at the back of the growing mob caught his attention. People parted and a lone figure in riding breeches, white billowing shirt and shining boots marched toward him.

Pulling a monogrammed handkerchief from his sleeve, the outsider whipped it across Morgan's cheek.

"I formally challenge you to a duel."

The corners of the night elf's lips curled in amusement. He pulled himself tall, staring directly at the man and replied.

"I accept your challenge." Turning to the crowd, he searched but was unable to see his sister. *Where is she?*

"Is there someone here who will act as the referee?"

"Didn't you pick one before now?" A raspy male voice from the gathered mob hollered.

Morgan drew himself to his full height. "There was no time."

"I'll referee." From the midst of people, a parting of the crowd showed a small being swathed in leather from head to toe and carrying a blade upon her back.

Morgan raised a brow and looked down his aquiline nose. "And who might you be?"

Tiamoon looked around at the gathering. She would need to be… cautious with her response.

"I'm Tia from the far side of the meadow. I have knowledge of dueling and can be an impartial referee."

Morgan let his eyes rove over the small creature standing before him. Should it decide against him, two swift swings of his blade could end this creature's existence and no one would be the wiser. *Why not?*

"I've no objection." He turned to his opponent. "And you?"

Florence blinked his eyes to be sure he was seeing the sight standing before him. His knowledge of the wee ones imparted to him in bedtime tales covered gnomes and as sure as he was standing here getting ready for a sword duel, this being was a gnome.

"I've no problem."

Morgan swung his blade with his wrist, twirling the shining metal past his shoulders.

"Shall we begin? I've provided you a weapon over there." He indicated with a jerk of his head toward the practice sword on the grass.

Tia strolled to the weapon and lifted the metal spear. She drew her thumb down the blade and turned to glare at the night elf.

"The blade is dull. You will give him a stone and allow him ten minutes to sharpen this weapon."

Morgan rummaged in his pocket and tossed a whetstone to his opponent.

"There. Ten minutes, no more."

Tia looked toward the crowd. "Is there someone with a watch?"

A hand went up.

"Please let us know when ten minutes has passed."

Shirring sounds of stone against metal and shuffling feet filled the air. The spectators soon began to mumble and fidget.

"Time!"

Florence looked up, a shadow of fear passing over his face. He regained his composure and walked to the blonde giant. He handed the stone to its owner.

"Thank you."

Morgan smirked. "You're welcome."

"Please make a large circle so the challengers have plenty of room to spare."

The crowd shuffled back, raising a dust cloud silhouetted in the twilight. When sufficient space had been acquired, Tia turned and looked at both men.

"Stand with your backs to each other."

When the two competitors were back to back, it was clear Morgan had the advantage of height and arm length.

In the crowd, Dorinda watched in horror and wrung her hands.

Leaning against a tree behind the majority of the gawkers, Gitty propped one leg up against the trunk. Her line of vision was unimpaired by the shorter townsfolk.

Cary settled on her shoulder, her eyes popping at the sight of the opponent. What the devil had Florence done now?

"Are they really going to fight with swords?"

"Looks like it."

Good heavens! Fool was going to get himself killed! He was better with a firearm than a blade. Unfortunately, all she could do was sit back and observe.

"Who do you think will win this?"

"Oh, Morgan will make quick work of this. You watch."

Cary fretted for a moment then settled to study the duel. Florence had been given his chances. After all, wasn't the fault his they were stuck here?

The referee continued.

"Please take five paces. One...two...three...four...five. Now turn and face each other."

Morgan whisked around and looked into concerned brown eyes. He could sense fear from the intruder. *As well he should be.* He pulled his weapon to the front and grasped the hilt with both hands. Quickly he covered the ground between himself and his opponent just as the man had put up the blade in front of himself.

Morgan swung down with crushing force pushing the blade to the ground, the clanging of steel on steel echoing between the darkening mountains.

Florence sucked air into his lungs. The fierce attack of this blonde giant had taken him by surprise. He shoved upward, catching the steel of the other man's sword and flinging it up toward the giant's shoulder.

The blonde warrior turned into the surprise move and jammed Florence's weapon up and over, catching the blade and flipping it from his hands. Morgan then pirouetted and ran the interloper through from front to back.

Shrieks and cries were all the gathered observers could do. On the ground, red staining the white shirt, lay the stranger.

Morgan walked to the edge of the meadow and wiped the blood from his steel. He'd do a careful cleaning when he returned home.

Dorinda burst through the throng and ran to her houseguest. She fell to her knees, gently cradling Florence's head in her lap.

He looked into her eyes and smiled weakly. Mouthing the words, thank you, he expelled his final breath.

She hovered her hand over his forehead and sensed the spirit had left his body. Lowering her head, she allowed tears to course down her cheeks.

Cary watched curiously from Gitty's shoulder then flew closer to observe the reaction of this other human. The female human was crying real tears over Florence. *How strange.* She, Cary, was supposed to be his guardian and, yet, she couldn't bring herself to feel sadness.

Winging her way back to the night elf, she realized she'd changed her alliances. This was the fate of her new life. Nothing ever stayed the same.

Gitty stood and straightened her leather jacket.

"I might as well congratulate Morgan. He'll be impossible if I don't."

The pair wended their way through the meandering crowd. As they neared the edge of the meadow, Cary's narrowed her eyes. *If I didn't know better…*

"Well, brother, you did well. Congratulations."

Morgan turned to face his sibling. "Where were you? I couldn't see you in the crowd. Did you catch the whole thing?"

"Yes, I saw the whole thing. I thought duels were supposed to be between equally matched opponents."

Morgan shrugged his shoulders as he leaned to pick up his blade.

"I can't help it if he chose the weapons. Point is I won. Thought I might head to the pub and have a beer or two. Care to buy me one?"

Cary dropped from Gitty's shoulder to the log holding the cape.

"Conn! You devil! Where have you been? Why weren't you

searching for Florence? Explain yourself!"

The male fae jumped from his perch at the bark of his name. He twisted around and winged backward.

"Cary! I, uh, I was looking for Florence." He pointed to the form lying recumbent on the ground. "See? I found him."

Cary punched him in the chest. "You idiot! How are we supposed to get home now?"

Conn winged his way above Morgan's shoulder. "I'm not sure I want to go home. What's there for us? More work? No thanks. I like where we are right now."

Gitty and Morgan looked at the two fae arguing.

"New friend, sister?"

Gitty bristled at Morgan's tone. "Yes. Just like yours. Useful and very devious. I see a way to get what we want without putting ourselves in danger."

Morgan slipped his blade into the scabbard and grabbed the cloak from the log.

"Tell me over a brew. I've worked up a thirst and I believe my small friend is in need also."

The siblings moved in the direction of the tavern while the wee folk continued their argument as they winged behind the night elves.

From behind a tree a small figure emerged.

I need to find out what they are up to before everything I know is destroyed.

Tiamoon pushed out a breath between her lips. She was going to have to go into the lion's den. If it meant saving her people, then so be it. The lion's den it was.

She set off toward town. This time tomorrow she would have the knowledge she needed to formulate a defense plan or die trying.

Chapter Seven

Darkening shadows stretched long across the valley. Tiamoon, lounging against her favorite oak casually swinging her blade, surveyed the meadow. Chills inched down her back, setting her nerves to tingling. Seeking solitude from the crush of the humans in the pub, she'd returned to observe the mortician's ministrations to the outsider. His body would reside in a pauper's grave. Tia could only hope his soul would find better accommodations.

Rocks crunching beneath boots alerted her to the approach of unwanted visitors. Two night elves deep in conversation strode her direction. She squinted her eyes and caught the flickering of wings from tiny fae surrounding the elves.

Tia felt her chest tighten. Faeries and night elves didn't normally mingle. *This doesn't bode well for the rest of us.* She leaned over and pulled her blade toward her as she slowly rose and slipped around the tree in sync with the night elves movement.

"What are you rambling on about, Morgan?" Gitty slowed her pace. "You're going to collect your practice sword, aren't you?"

Strolling to the red-stained metal shaft, he bent down to retrieve the implement. "Of course. We'll need every blade in the coming days. Weren't you listening at the last clan gathering?"

Cary and Conn, sensing a squabble brewing, flew themselves out of danger's range and hovered above the siblings.

Cary leaned toward Conn. "You smell of mead and tobacco. I thought you'd gone to search for Florence?"

Conn snapped his head her direction. "I was tracking him down. I can't help it if the journey took me to the pub, can I?"

Staring at the blood soaked ground; Cary wrinkled her forehead in consternation.

"Well, you did a slap-up poor job of finding him, now didn't ya?"

Conn noted her brogue deepening. If he didn't defend himself now, she'd start a railing that wouldn't stop until his ears bled.

"I located Morgan who let me know where Florence was to be. It's not my fault the fool went and issued a challenge he couldn't win. Besides, I was hungry and thirsty. What was I to do? Morgan was kind enough to offer me food and drink. Saying no would've been impolite."

Cary flew to inches in front of Conn's face. Gritting her teeth, she lowered her voice to just above a whisper. "You're his faerie godfather, Conn. Your responsibility was to guide him and watch over him. What about that?"

The fae straightened his back and reverse winged until he could look Cary in the eyes. "I guided him through his childhood. His decision to disregard my advice as a man had nothing to do with my efforts. I couldn't force him to use his common sense. Don't place the blame on me for his boastful nature. Florence developed that without my help and against my guidance."

Cary's wings slumped and she heaved a sigh. "Tis the truth. We can but lead them. We can't force them to use their knowledge. I'll give you that, Conn, but if I find you're only purpose in going to the pub was to quench your own thirst..."

He held up a hand. "On my honor as a fae godfather."

She eyed him suspiciously. *I've naught but to believe him.*

Their attention was drawn back to the night elf siblings sniping at each other.Gitty pulled her sword from the scabbard and twirled the blade, switching the fine steel claymore from hand to hand.

"Why should I listen? Most of the talk is you boys blowing your own horns about your conquests. I can live without knowing how many notches each of you has on your belts."

Tiamoon hunkered at the foot of the oak, her dark brown leather blending with the tree's bark coat. She keened her ears, held her breath and concentrated with all her being.

Morgan whipped around, covering the distance between himself and his sister with purposeful strides. His arm shot out and grabbed the twirling blade, yanking the weighty steel from her grasp. Standing toe to toe with his older sibling, he narrowed ice blue eyes at her.

"You arrogant ass. The council voted to interrupt the raids on the valley folk. Someone has gotten to them. They're talking about setting down a peace treaty with the locals. Do you really want to live on your little piece of land?

"We started this because we're far more intelligent than the local villagers and ruling is in our blood. Wasn't it your plan to own your own mountain and valley? Have you discarded that idea?"

Gitty placed her hand in the middle of his chest and shoved him.

"Don't ever get in my face like that again. I'll cut out your heart and feed it to you."

She snatched the saber dangling in Morgan's hand. Flipping it up and sheathing the metal, she walked toward the road then turned.

"I'll have my kingdom and you won't be allowed inside the borders." She tromped toward home, rising dust with each stamped footstep.

Morgan watched her ramrod straight back march away from him.

Cary sped up to catch Gitty.

Conn winged lazily to Morgan's side. "Is she going to be mad forever?"

Morgan jumped. "You startled me. No, she won't be mad forever, but being on Gitty's bad side is not good. I'd never tell her to her face but my sister is a formidable opponent. It's best when she's *got* my back, not trying to attack it. By the time she gets home, she'll come around to see things my way."

Morgan wiped the bloodied cutlass on the dew-laden grass until the blade appeared clean.

"What *are* you planning to do, if I may ask?" Conn cocked his head ever so slightly, frown wrinkles creasing his brow.

Morgan looked about the area.

Tiamoon held her breath and concentrated on trying to hear the night elf's plan.

Morgan meandered to the edge of the clearing and gazed at the meadow surrounded by forested mountains.

"This land is the richest I've ever seen. The local villagers are ignorant farmers and laborers with no knowledge of the wealth beneath their feet. So far, our clan has been able to flash a few gold coins in their eyes and buy up the property. The humans aren't the problem. This Depression they complain about has made them easy targets.

"No, it's the forest folk; the fae, gnomes, leprechauns, nymphs and sprites that are causing us the biggest concern. We need to run them out of the area. If they can't pay taxes, they can't live on the land. But the little blighters have dug in and won't be chased away."

Morgan turned to Conn. "Your people are very tenacious, little partner. Maybe you can offer me insight into a way to get them to leave?"

"Uh, I, uh, will have to put my mind to the task. Let me think it over and I'll get back to you."

Morgan leaned over and picked up his practice cutlass. "Don't take too long. We're planning a raid in the next few days and I want to be certain I'll have success. Before the next moon, I will own all my eyes can see."

He set a fast stride down the same path Gitty had taken, the little fae winging frenetically to keep pace.

Tiamoon counted to twenty then emerged from her hiding spot. Things were far worse than she'd imagined. She needed to rally her clans and pull in as many of the fae and others as she could.

She slid her blade in its casing on her back and trotted down the road toward her home. As she neared the cottage, she smelled the sweet wood her mother burned in the fireplace. Tia vaulted over the gate and burst through the front door.

"Mum, mum!"

Stirring a vessel on the potbellied wood stove, Skye started at the noisy intrusion.

"Why in the world are you yelling? Slow down, Labhoise, and take off your boots. You're tracking in mud all over my clean floor."

Sitting at the table looking a sight better than Tia had seen him in two days was Thomas who quirked an eyebrow and one corner of his mouth her direction.

"Labhoise?"

Before the last syllable had left his lips, a blade with razor-honed steel was at his throat. He gulped, feeling the cold steel prick his skin.

"Yes. It is my name but will never be uttered by the likes of you. If I find you have spoken this to anyone in this forest, you won't be able to tell anyone of your stash of gold.

"Are we clear?"

Thomas slowly moved his head up and down.

Tia removed the blade from his throat and propped it in the corner. She sat on a three-legged wooden stool by the fire's side and removed her boots, wiggling her toes to bring warmth to them. She gazed at the crackling flames, sagging on the small settee. Her simple life was getting too complicated and all of the problems pointed to the interlopers in the valley: the night elves.

Skye, her warring leathers traded for the comfort of a house smock, stirred the vegetable stew. Glancing at her daughter, she sensed unease in the young woman.

"What bothers you, daughter? What creates such deep longing and confusion?"

Tia stood and turned her back to the fire's warmth. She clasped her hands behind her and rocked lightly on the balls of her feet.

Nodding in Thomas' direction, she questioned. "Has he had any of the spirit today?"

Skye narrowed her eyes at the leprechaun.

"Not as far as I can tell. I upturned his flask in the sink and have kept a close eye on him while he was here."

Thomas shot a thunderous glare at Tiamoon. "I'm as bloody sober as I ever want to be, thanks to you. Can't say much for the condition."

"Good." She walked to the table and sat opposite Thomas, indicating her mother should sit.

"What I have is news...not good at best, disastrous at worst."

The frown melted from Thomas' face and Skye leaned toward her daughter.

"Wha-what news?" Thomas' voice shook and his lip began to quiver.

"Quit thinking of yourself, Leprechaun. This news will affect all the inhabitants of the valley."

Skye held up a hand. "If this is serious, I need to have my pipe to think. Thomas, would you care to indulge?"

"Yes, ma'am."

Tia huffed out an impatient breath. She tolerated her mother's smoking but wasn't an indulger herself, never having developed the taste for it.

After Skye and Thomas had packed and lit the long ebony carved pipes, Tia began to relate the information she'd gleaned from the night's reconnaissance as the other two settled in to listen.

Wispy tendrils of fragrant smoke curled above their heads. Skye and Thomas kept the pipes clenched tightly between their teeth and refrained from commenting.

"What I'm about to tell you came directly from a night elf known as Morgan. He and his sister reside in the abode on the top of the hill that overlooks the valley. To this point, they've caused little problems...or so we thought.

"I've just learned they are buying up as much of the land from the humans as they can. Somehow, they have gold when others do not. They aren't worried about the humans. They are worried about the valley folk.

"Morgan mentioned the other clans have become tired of warring and are happy to settle with what they've received from the humans. He, on the other hand, wants as much land as he can get and domination over the entire valley: magic *and* nonmagic folk.

"He's making plans to raid in the next few days. He wants us gone before the set of the next moon."

Skye pulled deeply on her pipe. She appeared to be concentrating on a spot across the room. Slowly, smoke trickled from her mouth, lazily clinging to her burnished red hair.

"I've been part of the talks with the night elves."

Tia raised her eyebrows.

Skye pulled the pipe from her mouth and pointed it at her daughter.

"It's not necessary for me to tell you everywhere I go. You were busy patrolling the valley.

"At the last meeting, we'd come to an agreement to sign a treaty. If the young bucks have taken it in their minds to start raiding, I think it's time to call in the head of their clan. The elder night elves are tired of the warring and wish to settle on the lands they have now. There's enough for all of us to live without encroaching on the other's territory.

"I must think on this, daughter. It's time for dinner."

"Food?" Thomas put his pipe on the table and rubbed his hands together. "Sounds good to me!"

"Bah! All you think about is your stomach." Tia got up and grabbed the bowls and spoons. Maybe her brain would work better if her stomach were full.

It couldn't work any worse.

Chapter Eight

Shuffling sounds filled the room as participants from the clans settled at the table. One side of the long wooden slab seated heads from the night elves; facing them were the gnome, faerie, leprechaun and wood nymph clan leaders.

Skye stood and cleared her throat.

"I want to thank everyone for attending tonight. We have much to discuss. I'll get directly to the point. Are all the clans represented?"

She watched a familiar figure rise across the table from her, his white hair flowing around his muscular shoulders.

"All the representatives of the night elf clans are here." The smooth baritone of the speaker reverberated in the room.

Skye swallowed hard. *I have to keep my mind on the proceedings.* She pulled in a calming breath.

"Thank you, Aethel. I think we can achieve our goals quickly so we can all go to our homes before the sun rises this time." A shy smile covered her face.

Ahhh! That man makes my knees go wobbly.

Aethel stepped around his chair, moving to the head of the table.

"What is so urgent we need to meet three days prior to our scheduled time?"

Skye moved so she was opposite the clan leader. Her palms had begun to sweat and she knew if he got too close he'd be able to see her heart pounding wildly in her chest.

Pulling to her full four foot eleven inch height, Skye plunged ahead.

"Are you aware within the last rising and setting of the sun a human was killed by a night elf?"

43

Stunned expressions and crushing silence was her answer.

Skye avoided looking directly at Aethel. Her eyes connected with the other clan leaders as she continued. "A young night elf known to frequent the meeting places of the humans engaged in an altercation with a newcomer to the valley. Their verbal sparring peaked in a duel challenge."

Whispers morphed to murmurs and the participants at the table sent furtive glances toward Aethel, whose flushed face belied the straight line of his lips and determined set of his jaw.

"The humans gathered last evening in the meadow next to their drinking place. When the challenge had been dealt and accepted, two figures stood in a circle of witnesses.

"It's my understanding the actual duel was brief; the night elf dispatching his opponent painlessly and quickly."

Aethel pulled out the chair at the head of the table and dropped onto the wooden seat. A vein on the side of his neck visibly throbbed.

"When the duel ended, the humans went to their pub and continued as though nothing had occurred. Their keeper of the dead came out and took away the remains. What happened next is of concern to each and every council member here."

Skye paced the floor, biting the side of her lip and contemplating how to cautiously phrase her next thought.

"A conversation was heard between the victor of the duel and a female night elf."

Aethel's shoulders flinched.

"The young night elf boasted of a raid to be staged in the next few days. The tone of his comments indicated we have young ones not willing to listen to the judgment of their elders. He spoke of power, possession and domination of all creatures of the valley.

"If this is indeed the climate of feeling among the young warriors, we could be facing dire consequences."

Skye looked around the room and noted each clan member deep in thought. It wasn't a comforting sight.

"I'm asking for your solutions to stop this bloodshed before it happens."

"You're wrong."

She looked up to face the voice of dissention.

"What makes you say that, Glade?"

The night elf of the woods clan stood and peered down his straight nose at the gnome leader.

"I have spoken to my clansmen, young and old, and they tire of the constant threat of war. Many of the young men are seeking to settle and raise families. Who is your source for this outrageous story?"

Skye gritted her teeth. Glade was known to be argumentative. Sometimes, she thought, just for the sake of arguing.

"I don't wish to speak the name."

"There you have it." Glade slapped his hand on the wooden tabletop. "If you won't reveal your source, how are we to know what has been spoken is the truth? Maybe you're making this up to catch us off guard and attack us." He shrugged his shoulders. "Who knows? Unless you can provide a witness to this conversation, we only have the word of a...gnome."

The curl of Glade's lip left no doubt about his feelings.

The door to the meeting hall slammed shut.

All heads turned toward the sound.

"You dare to call the head of my clan a liar?" A young male gnome planted his feet shoulder width apart, sword drawn and at the ready.

Skye turned to the figure. "Terran, please. The man is entitled to his opinion."

The gnome Terran strode to Skye's side. "Aye, he is, but not when he fouls the clan's honor."

The night elf Glade yanked his sword from the casing and, in two swift steps, stood next to the gnomes, weapon in hand, towering dangerously over the two.

Aethel rose, his chair scraping across the floor. He threw out his arm, toppling the cutlass from Glade's hand.

Whipping quickly around, right hand fisted and swinging, Glade's dark green eyes sparked as Aethel caught the thrown punch mid-air.

"Glade." Aethel's low warning held menacing undertones.

The night elf of the woods clan wrenched his hand to his side.

"This is not over, Aethel. You may head this council, but I don't recognize your authority and won't be bound by the decisions made here."

He leaned in and dropped his voice. "Prepare yourself and your little friends. I believe Morgan has the right idea and I may consider joining his campaign."

Stepping away, he gave a quick jerk of his head. Chairs dropped to the floor of the meeting hall as several clan leaders jumped up, clomping their boots and banging the doors on their way out.

Skye pivoted on her heel and headed for the door. Hesitating at the exit, she twisted to face the rest of the clan members shuffling to leave the table.

"I think we'll need to regroup and meet at another time. I'll send messages via the mouse network. Everyone take care when traveling homeward. Tonight has shown we've come no further than we were a year ago. Terran, we head for our home. Aethel...good to see you again."

Skye acknowledged the night elf with a quick head bob. She left the meeting hall and slipped the dagger from her belt, hiding it up the sleeve of her shirt. Terran trotted behind, his hand on the hilt of his blade, surveying the landscape in all directions. In a complete reversal of previous congresses, tonight's meeting put the council back to where each clan had stood at the very first get together, and Skye no longer felt safe in her land.

She feared a bloodbath was about to ensue, regardless of the careful negotiations accomplished to this point. There really was nothing as headstrong as a young man trying to prove himself to the world.

Skye tread lightly, scanning the surrounding meadow and woods as she moved toward home on soft leather boots.

Terran, straining to hear beyond the hushed footfalls of Skye, brought up the rear; walking in the same spots.

Skye was deep in contemplation. She'd fallen for persistent attention lavished on her when she'd been but a young warrior. A tall, elegant white-haired night elf had stolen her heart and sweet-talked her into ignoring the common sense whispering in her ears. Furtive meetings in dense forest locations had produced many memorable nights...and a daughter. The night elf had disappeared out of Skye's life as quickly as he'd appeared.

It wasn't until many years later she'd learned of his arranged marriage to the daughter of a chieftain, putting an end to generations of warring between the clans. The woman quickly gave birth to two children: a daughter and a son, expiring while giving the son life.

She felt blessed her daughter resembled her and not the father, making explanations unnecessary.

Skye and Terran reached the cottage. Smoke spiraled from the chimney and a candle glowed in the window.

"We're welcomed," Skye whispered.

"Good, I'd hate to have to fight my way back in my own home."

Skye could tell her son was smiling. Joy bubbled through his voice.

A quick entrance and the two warriors stood inside the living room. Thomas, the leprechaun, was snoring in the armchair facing the fire, his feet stretched in front of him, pipe smoldering in the abalone shell on the side table. Tiamoon sat on the three-legged stool, gazing into the fire.

"Hello, daughter."

She swiveled on her seat to acknowledge her mother when she caught sight of another figure skulking in the shadows of the room.

"Who's there?" She sprung from the stool clamping her hand on the fireplace poker and wielding the implement as a weapon.

The figure chuckled then burst into laughter.

"Do you know how silly you look, sister?"

Tia glared at the figure until his words connected with her brain.

"Terran?" Tia set the poker against the flagstone hearth. "Is it really you?"

The young gnome stepped into the glowing ring of light cast by the fire.

"Yes, sister. It's me."

Tia quickly covered the floor space and smothered her brother in a hug.

"When did you arrive? What have you found out? How many bought swords are we facing?"

Terran wiggled free from her grasp and held up his hand. "Whoa, big sis. Let me unstrap my weapon and sit in front of the fire. My body is tired from the journey. I wish a warm cup of mother's broth and to remove my boots."

"I'll get you the broth and some bread but you're on your own for taking off your boots." Tia wrinkled her nose, much to Terran's delight.

"It's good to see little has changed since my leaving." Setting in the other armchair facing the fire, he ripped the bread into pieces and dipped a piece in the broth, bringing both to his mouth. Eyes closed in delight; he swallowed and released a long sigh.

"I have missed this."

Skye slipped to her room. The children could update her with the latest news in the morning. The council meeting had tried her patience and worn her out. There was also the matter of seeing Aethel again. It had been many a year, but her heart still skipped a beat and her stomach hurt every time she spotted the night elf. A good night's rest would put things back into perspective.

~ * ~

Tia watched as her brother gorged himself on the broth. When he had finished and removed his boots, she drew the stool next to his chair.

"What have you found, brother?"

Terran stared at the flames dancing in the hearth.

"The threat we've suspected is real-very real. There is a faction of night elves determined to rule this valley. They have enlisted the help of mercenaries from afar and make plans in the dark of the night. The elder clansmen have no knowledge of the plans or the mercenaries. I think we're on our own."

Tia used the poker to shove the logs in the grate around then added a new one on the dying stack. Flames flared up, expelling heat and light.

"What are we to do, Terran?"

Brother and sister stared into the fire.

"Nothing tonight. I'm exhausted and can't think clearly. After a good night's sleep, I'll tackle this problem again."

Tia rose and strolled to her room. Terran was right. The evening had dragged and Thomas' constant whining about not having any liquor to drink had worn on her. She was no good to anyone at this moment. Sleep, indeed, appeared to be the best idea.

Chapter Nine

Wan flaxen rays of sunlight reached across diaphanous pillows of fog covering the dew-laden meadow. Gitty stood holding her coffee cup, staring at the light playing off the mist. Steam curled around her nose, wafting the pungent smell of freshly ground coffee beans to her olfactory senses.

Before her lay the fertile meadow gently sloping up to the velvet green mountains covered in usable forests. A smile touched her lips. *My meadow, my forests.*

Oh, yeah. Morgan might have illusions of power, but Gitty would guarantee the reality of ruling. From what she had ascertained about the meeting last night in the few mumbled words her father had spoken as he had stomped past her to his bedroom, the peace committee had been disrupted and temporarily put on hold. It was her duty to make sure the treaty was never signed.

Morgan stumbled into the living room and through to the kitchen. Several minutes later, Gitty heard him plop himself on the settee.

"Tough night, little brother?" Gitty turned to face him.

Squinting up at her, he grunted.

"Aren't you just the picture of polite conversation today?"

Morgan gulped a large mouthful of coffee. "Better things to do than make small talk with you. I've an important meeting to attend. I'll be out all day."

Gitty raised a brow. "Really. Since when do you leave the house before 4 pm?"

Morgan rose from the couch, grabbed his cup and tromped toward the hallway.

"I haven't time the time to argue, Gitty. My future is something I plan to mold myself, and I have an appointment with destiny."

Gitty blew out an exasperated breath and rolled her eyes. "Dragons and trolls, Morgan. I've barely had time to down my coffee and you're spouting rhetoric worthy of Shakespeare. You must've been drinking tainted mead, for it's surely gone to your head."

She looked around the room, noting she'd not seen Cary since storming from the meadow last evening. Had the tiff between the siblings frightened the little fae?

Gitty shrugged her shoulders. While the little fae was a welcome diversion and having her as a spy in the faerie camp would give Gitty a huge advantage, she'd done fine before the wee one appeared on the scene.

Morgan appeared and moved toward the back door. He was attired in the clan's red-brown colors; a dark brown cloak about his shoulders, black polished riding boots on his feet. His hair was tied back with a dark brown leather strip and he carried his fighting steel.

"I'm taking a horse from the stables. And Gitty," Morgan turned to face his sister, "I wouldn't go out after dark."

He departed before she could reply. Moving back to the window, she watched him gallop down the driveway on his brown steed. Out of the corner of her eye, she spied the tiniest distortion in the air. Peering to the valley, she scrutinized each inch of the scene below her. As she was about to give up and get more coffee, the air directly in front of her wavered.

Gitty sucked air to her lungs. *There's old magic here. If the Ancient Ones have been brought in, Morgan and his friends could be in trouble. Heck, we'll all be in deep trouble.*

Aethel ambled through the living room and toward the kitchen, dark circles under his blue eyes. He grabbed a cup from the cupboard and poured coffee for himself. Sitting at the kitchen dinette, he spooned two teaspoons of sugar into the black concoction and stirred.

Gitty slipped in behind him and watched as he dropped his head to his hands. "Are things alright, Father?"

Aethel groaned. "No. Did you know your brother was involved in a duel last night?"

His question echoed through the room. He lifted his head and looked into the guilty eyes of his daughter. "As I suspected...you knew and you were there. Before you try to deny it, there were witnesses."

"Who says I was going to deny it?"

"Your brother and his renegade friends will be the death of us all. I've spent the night tossing and turning with the knowledge we are one step from war with the humans. We can't afford war with the humans. And if that isn't enough, my senses tell me there is Old Magic being used close by.

"My skin is crawling from the spell casting."

Gitty went to the stove and pulled out a frying pan. She collected eggs from the icebox and sliced bread from the breadbox. Muttering under her breath, she proceeded to magic the eggs to cook and bread to toast. Fixing the food on the plate, she handed it to her father.

"Thank you. This should help."

"Why are you so determined *not* to war with the humans? We're superior to them in every way and should control this entire valley, not the other way around. They should be trying to get along with us." Gitty dropped her long frame into a chair opposite her father.

"The world doesn't always work the way you think it should, daughter. You must remember we're visitors here."

"Not if we own all the land."

Aethel looked up from his food. "If the humans don't wish to sell to us, how do you propose we get ownership of the land?"

She leaned back in the chair and looked at the ceiling, her mind churning, as she formulated a non-confrontational answer.

"Magic."

The clattering of the fork on the china plate rang through the kitchen.

"You would magic the inhabitants to turn over their land to you? What about when they awoke from the spell? What then?" Aethel's eyes had turned a steely gray as he fixed an angry glare on his daughter.

Gitty stared at her father. *What's happened to the fearless warrior of yesteryear who'd peered into the jaws of death and charged ahead anyway?*

"By the time these witless wonders came around, we'd own their property and they'd have to pay taxes to live on it. We'd be the rightful rulers of this land. What else matters?" She furrowed her brow in disbelief.

Aethel stood, set his plate in the kitchen sink and magicked it clean then turned to his offspring.

"Take yourself elsewhere for the day. I'm not sure I can control my anger enough *not* to destroy you. Don't show your face to me until the rise of the sun tomorrow." Fists clenched against his side, Aethel stomped from the kitchen.

Gitty smirked. *Just as well.* She retired to her room and rummaged in her clothing chest. Many months had passed since she'd ridden her horse. Today would be a perfect time to remedy the situation. She pulled the white chaps from the chest and lashed them on, grabbing her long duster and a white hat in case the skies opted to dump rain on her.

She tromped to the back porch and sat on a wooden chair, slipping into her riding boots. The night elf craftsman who'd created her gear had spent many months bleaching the leather to a sparkling white. Gitty had demanded the leathers be created the old way, by hand, not by magicking the material to the desired color.

She slammed the door and strode to the stables, covering the quarter acre quickly in her fury. Her father had grown weak in his time in this inconsequential valley, but she had not. She'd watched him succumb to the taming imposed by the council. No night raids for him, no. He'd sat by the fire reading the old texts, trying to apply their wisdom to the new situation.

She could have told him it wouldn't work but he didn't want to hear it.

Gitty swung up on the finely crafted saddle and yanked the reins to the bit of her mare, directing the animal to the driveway running by the castle. The sooner she was away from here the better. She touched her pouch to ensure there were coins for necessities. A quick kick to the mare's flanks and she galloped away from the mountain's top. By the time she returned, her plan would be set in motion, father or no father.

~ * ~

Conn rubbed his hands together and flew loop-de-loops in delight.

Cary pumped her wings, feeling the lack of use in her shoulder blades.

"Why are you so happy? I'm tired, hungry and I want to sleep in my own bed. I can sense we're close to the place we settled in but I'm not completely sure I can find it. Will you stop acting foolish and get us home?" She scowled Conn's direction.

"There's going to be a wa-a-a-r-r-r. There's going to be a wa-a-a-a-r-r-r."

Cary stopped mid-air, hovering. She grabbed Conn's arm and jerked him around to face her.

"You're an idiot. Don't you remember the last time these humans fought? There was bloodshed all around us. We nearly lost everyone we cared about!"

"Pshaw! This time the magical folks will win and these humans will be gone. We'll have control of the meadows and forests again." Conn danced a jig.

"CONN!!"

He stopped and turned to stare at Cary.

"What is your problem? This is good news for us all."

"You've been listening to that Morgan elf. *We* aren't from here. *We* know nothing about these humans, this land, the night elves...need I go on?"

Conn floated, winging lazy circles around Cary. "I have been listening to Morgan and I agree with him. The Others here are very backward. They're nearly the same as the Others we left back home. How could we not succeed here? Once the night elf clans conquer the valley, we'll have free reign to do what we want. Isn't it great?"

He zipped up and turned somersaults in the air.

Cary moved in the direction she thought the oak where they were staying grew. "All I want is to go home to Ireland. This place is different. They talk funny and no one really believes in us here. I'm homesick and I want to go home. I don't want to see these Others kill each other over pieces of land."

Conn shrugged his shoulders. He'd never really understood Cary's love of the land. Oh, sure, he loved his Ireland, but this land was green and there was much to be gained by starting new. Maybe he could conjure that big red travel thing which had brought them here. If he could just remember the conjuring spell...

~ * ~

Aethel sat on the ledge of his bedroom window peering in the direction of the meadow. He couldn't shake the image of Skye from his mind. She'd aged, but then so had he and she'd apparently married, as had he. The young warrior Terran, with firm jutting jaw, straight back and tenacity reminded Aethel so much of Skye, he'd bet his best stallion the young gnome was her son.

He found his heart aching with the need to touch her again and flinching a bit in jealousy. What would have happened had the two of them mated? Ah, but these were the meanderings of a lifelong past. It could never happen. Night elves married and mated with night elves and gnomes married and mated with gnomes. Some lines weren't crossed. It didn't matter if he'd loved Skye. There, the truth had been revealed.

Sure, his wife had been tall, lean and elegant, just like Gitty. Unlike Gitty, his Ella had possessed a kind heart and they'd grown to appreciate each other, but Aethel had not loved Ella. It saddened him to lose her when Morgan was born.

Seeing Skye again brought a rush of feelings he'd thought dead. Oh well, not much he could do now. Because of his two renegade children, the valley and its inhabitants, including Skye and her family, were in great danger.

Aethel stood and looked over the meadow. They might think him old...but it was up to him to prove them wrong and save the valley from their arrogance. He might have propagated them but he didn't have to like them.

It was a sad fact, but Aethel's children had become his enemy, and he was determined to win this war. More than the night elves and gnome lives depended on his success.

Chapter Ten

Everything about the scene before her was wrong. Scorched spots blackened the earth and marred nearby trees. Splintered branches littered the ground and the scuffmarks crisscrossing the forest floor hinted at recent activity. Reaching over her shoulder, she guided the tempered blade from its leather encasement and held the weapon in front of her.

The air wavered and Tiamoon froze in place, holding her breath. The flesh on her arms rose and hair on the back of her neck prickled. Magic had been used here recently. She moved leather-clad feet slowly, silently around the edge of the scuffed area. Her lungs ached for air and the side of her lip pulsed where she clamped down with her teeth.

Tia poked the shrubbery with her blade. Under a mulberry leaf, wings crumpled beneath a tiny body, lay an inert fae of the wood clan. Tia let go the breath she was holding. The sight was worse than she could possibly have imagined. Moving quickly, she reconnoitered the area and discovered eleven dead fae and one barely clinging to life.

She placed her blade on the ground and knelt at the male fae's side. "Who did this to you?" She placed a leaf over the tiny one's body.

Very faintly, the male whispered. "Morgan."

She leaned her ear close to his mouth. "Who?"

"Morgan."

Buzzing about her head alerted her she was not alone. Again the annoying buzz sounds, and now, pinpricks of pain. Tiamoon tried tracking the sound with her eyes. Just when she thought she'd determined the source, a stab of pain would distract her.

"Stop! I'm not sure why you've targeted me but stop. I'm not the enemy."

She stood still as the oaks growing nearby, listening as the buzzing slowed to the swishing sounds of many tiny wings.

Two male fae flew to the front of her face and pointed lances her direction.

"Do not move, gnome. We've seen the damage you've inflicted here." The speaker swept an arm at the lifeless bodies scattered on the ground. "You may have had the upper hand with my kinfolk but I bring reinforcements and we won't be so blindly trusting."

Tia watched as a multitude of faeries appeared before her eyes. She sheathed her sword. Slow, measured steps took her to a stump where she opted to sit and allowed the emotion of the sight she'd stumbled upon to overtake her. A tear meandered down her cheek.

"Such waste; such destruction. Your poor kinfolk had no chance. This is the work of the night elves. I can only guess they stunned your warriors and dispatched them with no conscience."

The male faes darted looks at each other and continued to hold their lances on the seated gnome.

"You lie. You're trying to divert attention from yourself from the heinous act of murder!"

Multitudes of wings fluttered with the murmured agreement of the crowd.

Tia stood. "No. I was searching to find the elves before something like this occurred. I'm trying to stop them. Everyone in the valley will be in danger if they gain the upper hand and take over.

"I've no quarrel with you. I think we need to join forces against the night elves. If all the forest and meadow folk get together in a united front, we can make sure the valley stays ours. If we don't, we'll be subject to the whims of the night elves."

The two male fae lowered their lances and winged backward.

Tia watched as they drew several others from the throng and conferred among themselves. She could only hope her argument was strong. It was difficult to gauge the fae community. For the most part, they were very unreliable, concerned only with life's enjoyments. But many were deceived by this attitude and knew not what fearsome warriors they could be when their homes were endangered. Most magic had been gifted to others by the fae. The extent of their magical understanding had never been tested.

Tiamoon was not about to be the first to test the depths.

The two male fae winged to her, their lances, once again, pointed her direction.

"We can't trust your word. All we know is we came to help our kinsmen but found most of them dead and you hovering over the last one breathing. Your prowess with a sword is legend, gnome. It's not beyond reason to think you inflicted all this destruction.

"We will handle our own affairs and take care of our own families. It might be in your best interest to leave this valley. Word will spread and you won't be welcomed in any community."

Tia clenched her fists at her side. "Do you threaten me, fae?"

The throng of faeries buzzed forward pointing weapons her direction.

"Fine. I offered my sword to you and you refused. Don't call on me when you find yourselves under the grinding boots of the night elves. I take my leave."

She turned her back on the warriors, leaving and keeping to the edge of the woods. Her heart pounded and she ran a tongue over her dry lips. She was in a precarious position. The night elves would run roughshod over the inhabitants of the valley if something wasn't done, but her offer of services had met with rejection.

The fae community was suspicious of all outsiders, a fact Tiamoon knew. But she'd relied on her being part of the magical folk of the area to help her win their trust, an obvious mistake. This valley was in for a war like no other and everyone, except the night elves, stood to lose.

I'm not sure I can stand by and watch my people get slaughtered.

A solution was needed and soon. At the moment, Tiamoon wanted to get home without becoming the next victim in the fray.

~ * ~

Gitty galloped her stallion across the meadow to the edge of the verdant forest opposite her home. An old ally had been rumored to be in the area. Slowing her steed to a walk, she kept herself vigilant. The old growth woods could shield many an opponent. Her horse tugged at the reins and snorted impatiently. Halfway up the first hill, the stallion stopped and could not be coaxed to move one step further.

Gitty kicked his flanks but the beast would not budge. In an angry huff, she flung her right leg over the saddle and dismounted, turning to stare down the shaft of a highly sharpened sword. Startled ice-blue eyes rose to gaze into deep green orbs.

"Glade." The whispered name floated through the air.

"You'd best be careful, Gitty. Next time, your opponent might not be as taken with a blonde, blue-eyed amazon." His lips curled into a smile that reached his eyes.

He lowered his weapon and stepped forward, gathering her in his arms and crushing her lips beneath his.

Gitty sucked in a deep draught of air when he released her.

"What makes you think I wanted that?" She furrowed her brows at him.

A deep bubbling sound echoed beneath the forest's green canopy.

"Because, my love, you didn't fight me in the least and I still hold you in my arms."

She tried to wiggle free but the arms holding her gently tightened as her captor pulled her close.

"I won't lose this opportunity to make up for lost time, love."

Glade lowered his lips and stopped just above hers.

Gitty waited but he moved no further. When she could stand it no longer she reached up and closed the space between them, slipping her arms around his neck.

He groaned deep in his throat as she pulled from him.

"It has been too long Gitty Saun, too long. I've missed your sharp tongue and quick wit. But most of all I've missed holding you in my arms. How have you been?"

"After all these years you ask now, Glade? Where did you go? Why didn't you contact me? You could have magicked a message to me. What happened?"

The dark-haired night elf pulled back, grabbed the reins of the horse and slipped his arm around the blonde amazon's waist.

"This is not a safe haven. I'll explain once we've arrived at camp."

He led her through a maze of trees and bushes, paths twisting, turning and doubling back on themselves. Just about the time Gitty felt truly lost, the thick forest opened to reveal a camp with many traveling caravans.

Curious eyes watched the striking couple enter the campsite.

Glade led the stallion and Gitty to a wooden caravan. Brightly painted designs covered the outside. Stairs descended from the door to the forest's floor and Gitty noted the wooden wheels were covered in rubber. Glade tied the steed to the side of the vehicle near a filled water bucket. He slid his hand beneath Gitty's arm and directed her to the caravan's door.

"Go inside. I'll bring hay for your stallion and give him a quick brushing."

Gitty turned to protest but Glade had disappeared.

She climbed the steps and entered the box on wheels. Surprised at the space within, she sat at a table and looked out a portal to the outside. The floor of the caravan was covered in hand woven rugs. Colorful pillows dotted the table benches and hurricane lamps hung from metal hooks protruding from the walls.

Glade came through the opening and slid next to her.

"What do you think of my home?"

"This is your home?"

"Has been for the last twenty years."

"I thought your family had a castle in the old country."

Glade heaved a sigh, his shoulders drooping. "We did. For millennia we had a castle with lands, rivers and towns. But the last one-hundred-fifty years have taken their toll on our land and clan. With more than a dozen wars happening, the last World War causing the most damage, my people have had to flee our homeland."

"Couldn't you just fight back?"

"We have magic like you but these humans, these Others, have weapons so destructive we were outmatched. Before we could organize and protect our lands, they had bombed the earth from beneath us. We fled over the North Pole and through Canada to come back here. Some of our southern cousins recalled these caravans from the early wandering night elves and created them for us here. They're mobile and contain all we need to survive. They'll do."

Gitty looked around. A shy smile touched her lips. "Yes, they will."

Glade gazed at her porcelain face. "Gitty, my love?"

"Hhmm?"

"What is it you want from me?"

She turned wide eyes on him. "What makes you think I want something?"

Glade burst into laughter. "Because I know you. We had a great love--once--but I've never known you to pine for a man, and *need* is not in your vocabulary."

Gitty felt heat rush to her cheeks. She hated it when Glade foresaw her every move. It was one of the reasons she'd walked away from him. He knew her too well.

"Okay, fine. My brother Morgan is gathering troops around him for a takeover of the valley."

"I was aware he was purchasing land from the Others at a rapid pace but I didn't know he was serious about a war."

Gitty nudged him to move and scooted from the table to pace the small room.

"I'm not really sure he wants to go to war but he wants to appear powerful so others will respect him."

"That's a dangerous undertaking, isn't it?" Glade frowned.

"Yes and he has no experience commanding anybody, let alone a bunch of young night elves out for blood."

Glade leaned back and crossed his arms. "So why are you so concerned? You have no love for the humans of your valley?"

Gitty turned a lopsided grin his direction. "Because *I* want to control the valley and I *do* have experience commanding a group of blood-thirsty night elves."

He chuckled. "Aye, you do. Well, Gitty, my love, would it be worth my skin?"

She tilted her head and looked at him from beneath her eyelashes.

"Aye, Glade, aye."

Chapter Eleven

Smoke curled lazily from the chimney as Tiamoon padded toward home. She could only hope Thomas had decided to leave and quit living off the kindness of her mother.

The gate creaked as she opened it, reminding her yet again of the need to oil the hinges. She pushed open the cottage door and was met with the spicy aroma of mulled cider. Her stomach growled and Tia made for the stool by the fire.

She shed herself of the blade and scabbard, standing them next to the hearth before sitting to peel off her boots and stick her feet near the fire. *What am I to do?*

A hand reached around and placed a mug of the warmed cider in her grasp.

Tia turned and looked up at her mother. "Thanks."

"What troubles you, daughter?"

She sipped from the cup and contemplated.

"I came across a scene so horrific today, I can barely think on it."

Skye felt a shiver course down her back. "What would that be?"

"I set out to find the night elves. I'd heard from some of the river faeries Morgan and his cronies were traipsing through the woods destroying all in their path. I was wary, at first, but was forced to re-examine what I know about Morgan. He's no stomach for bloodshed, only for wooing the ladies.

"I started at the south woods and crept my way through the wood nymphs' glen. As I neared the woodland faeries home, I realized I couldn't hear any of the birds singing. No insects were buzzing and the air around me pressed heavy on my skin.

"I slowed my pace and silenced my footsteps. The ground in front of me was scorched and several trees had blackened spots on the bark. Branches lay broken on the ground. I let my eyes sweep the landscape and they fell on the most horrible of scenes. Scattered about the ground were dead faeries, their wings and clothes burnt, weapons scattered. I noted one male fae in front of me struggling to breath. I leaned down to see if I could help and he whispered one name...Morgan."

Tia looked up at her mother, eyes spilling tears. "Mum. They had no chance. Morgan killed them all! How could this happen in our valley?"

Skye dropped into the seat by the fire. *How, indeed.* She would have to find a way to contact Aethel and incorporate his help. The humans could be expected to fight and kill each other. It seemed to be what they did best, but the valley folk were better than that. They were supposed to get along and help each other. This… slaughter was unthinkable.

Skye placed her hand on her daughter's shoulder, feeling the young woman's body shake with emotion.

"Is there more to this, Labhoise?"

A deep sigh escaped the young gnome warrior. "Yes. They accused me of causing the deaths of the wee ones."

Blue eyes filled to the brim with tears looked pleadingly at Skye.

"How could they possibly think I would harm any of them? I offered to help them find Morgan, but they told me they didn't want my help and to stay away from them.

"Mum, what am I to do? I can't just stand by and let them be massacred."

Skye pulled Tia into her arms and held the young woman, stroking her red locks and allowing her to cry herself out.

"Whatever we attempt, child, we must do under cover of night. We'll protect our forest and meadow from those who would destroy the lands and us. This is not done. We won't lie down and let them annihilate us."

~ * ~

Dorinda gave the table one more swipe with the wet cloth and stepped around the back of the bar. Her keen eye noted the strange foreigners who'd started hanging out didn't come in as often as they once had.

The dandy Morgan was in almost every night, but all the others like him had quit appearing in her pub. She wasn't too disappointed. Oh, yeah, she liked the income, but the tall fair-haired men made the local boys nervous and caused more fights than she wanted to referee.

The women loved the attention but soon realized most of the foreigners had little or no money and were looking for a sugar mama.

It was while she'd been waiting to use the one restroom she'd heard the local females talking.

"Did you hear that braggart Morgan tonight?"

"No, what's he done now?"

"He was talking about buying the Thompson's farm. I didn't even know Bill and Joyce were selling. Did you?"

"No. Wait a minute. Didn't he say he'd bought the Williams' land last week?"

"Yeah. He did. What's he up to? He has enough money to buy a bunch of farms in the valley but can't buy his own drinks? I've had it with him. Beside, that new guy he brought in, the one called Glade? Well, he's really much cuter, anyway."

Dorinda stepped behind the door when the two women left the bathroom. She watched as they walked back to the restaurant. The news she'd just heard was very disturbing. She'd investigate first thing in the morning when the bank opened.

Morning arrived in a blaze of sunshine. Dorinda gazed out her kitchen window at glowing golden rays. She stood at the sink finishing the morning's dishes. With Mr. Florence gone, there were only two residents at her inn and and they were leaving this morning for Eugene. When she'd made mention she needed to do some banking in town, Mr. Jones offered to give her a lift to the city. She'd take the afternoon bus home and arrive in time to get the bar ready for the evening crowd, if there was one.

She donned her going-to-town dress and grabbed her spring hat. You could never be sure in the early months of the season if it would rain or not so Dorinda brought an umbrella and a slicker. She stopped by her desk and opened the business drawer, retrieving a slip of paper which she stuffed in her bag. Quick stepping to the front door, she locked the handle and crawled in the passenger seat of Mr. Jones' business coupe.

Conversation was polite and brief on the way in, each rider enjoying the passing scenery.

Dorinda thanked the gentleman when he dropped her at the bank, wishing him luck on his business trip and inviting him to stay at the inn should he pass that way again.

She straightened up and marched boldly through the front door and up to the receptionist.

"I'd like to see the president of the bank, please."

The older woman peered over her glasses at Dorinda and raised an eyebrow.

"May I ask what this is about?"

"No. I wish to discuss personal business with the president."

The woman rose from her seat and pointed at a straight-backed wooden chair positioned at right angles to the desk.

"Take a seat. I'll see if he's available."

Dorinda fretted with her umbrella, turning the handle in her fingers and chewing her bottom lip as she listened to the clicking sounds of the receptionist's heels on the bank's marble flooring. She noted the smell of Murphy's oil and let a smile slip to her lips. She used the same oil on the pub's bar top. She started at the brusque voice interrupting her thoughts.

"Mr. Clive will see you now."

The receptionist frowned as she pointed to the partially opened door titled 'President'.

Dorinda nodded at the receptionist. "Thank you."

One hour later, Dorinda emerged from the President's office, agitated at the news she'd discovered. She felt pushed by the urgency of the situation to contact all the farmers and businessmen in her town. A meeting had to be held as soon as she could possibly get people together. The face of the valley was changing and not in a positive way.

~ * ~

Glade sat up and stretched his arms. He'd have to remember to purchase material for the women to create more rugs for his floor. There wasn't much difference from the earth's ground and his caravan's rug covered wooden floor; both were hard and cold.

Rising up and quietly slipping out the door, he made his way to the stream to splash cold water on his face. His heart pounded wildly as he thought of the silken haired she-elf sleeping in his bed. Were he to settle into monogamy, Gitty would be his first choice. She, on the other hand, was only interested in power and had made that abundantly clear when they spoke last evening.

He'd watched her eyes glitter with the thought of owning the valley below this mountain, controlling all the inhabitants. He sucked in a breath when the ice-cold snow runoff hit his face. His whole body shivered as he splashed more water against his skin. He needed his wits about him this morning as he gathered his clan to share the decision he'd come to last night.

What he had said in the council meeting was true; his clan was tired of moving from place to place and desired nothing more than twenty or so acres away from the humans to create their own town and settle. What he was about to do was throw them into the heat of battle; the reward was the entire mountain. Once Gitty conquered all the other clans with his help and bought all the property the humans had, she would sit on her hill and rule as the queen she fancied herself.

"Morning, love."

Glade twisted to face the silver-haired night elf. Sunlight backlit her hair, casting a glow about her face.

"Morning. Did you sleep well?"

"Yes, but as I told you last night, you could have lain with me."

Glade smiled as he ran his hand down her cheek. "No. I will only lay with you if we are mated."

Gitty humphed. "That's not going to happen."

Glade grabbed the bottom of his tunic and blotted the excess water from his face.

"You made that brutally apparent last night. Where are you headed today?"

The pair moved in the direction of the base camp.

"I think I'll head to the village and start asking around. I'm sure there are some of the Others who haven't been approached by Morgan yet. If I can buy their land before he makes an offer, I'll be on my way to owning all I see."

Gitty leaned over and placed a kiss on Glade's cheek. "Good luck with your meeting today. I'll send a messenger bird with our next move. Thanks for the great night's sleep."

With the flash of a smile and wave of a hand, she swung up in the saddle of her stallion and reined him to leave the camp. Glade had magicked the directions back to the valley into the steed's ear the night before.

Glade watched her leave, a strange sensation settling over him. The sight of her back felt very final. He shivered and moved to the caravan. A good breakfast then a gathering of his clansmen. Today, they would begin their future.

Chapter Twelve

Dorinda got off the bus and scurried home. She had just enough time to start her letters to the local farmers. She knew ten days was almost too short to ask folks to come to a meeting, but the information she'd received at the bank put an urgency to her task. She gathered her writing tools. If business were slow tonight, she'd be able to get all the letters done and posted by tomorrow's mail.

The quiet life everyone once knew was about to go up in flames.

~ * ~

Skye sat at the head of the table; Aethel faced her from the opposite end. The last two weeks in the valley folk lives had taken a decided turn for the worse. Reports were trickling in from survivors of raids on outlying communities. Forest gnome clans, wood nymph clans and even the laconic leprechauns were taking up arms. The survivors straggled in to the meadow and collapsed in the homes of cousins.

After Skye's third cousin, a forest gnome, had stumbled to her cottage with news of total annihilation of two communities by night elves in forest green leathers, she called this emergency meet.

Tension filled the room and weapons rattled in nervous apprehension.

Skye stood. "Thank you all for taking the time from the protection of your homes to be here. I know most of you are not in the mood to talk peace but how about we talk cooperation?"

Protests passed among the seated participants and glares were directed Aethel's direction.

Skye called for silence. "We, too, have heard the stories from survivors, my own cousin, Etain from the forest clan, watched the invaders tear down her village and burn the trees. She heard them laugh about leveling the northern clan's homes. Had she not been hunting mushrooms, she would have perished."

The company of magical creatures rose from their chairs and moved Aethel's direction.

"Stop!" Skye held her blade with both hands in front of her, chair on the ground where she'd jumped up. "The next soul who moves will be cut in two."

"Why shouldn't we slice him in pieces and hang the bits from all the trees? It's *his* people who are doing this."

Skye inched forward. "Do any of you doubt my word?"

The room was filled with mumbles and grumbling.

"Then set yourselves down and listen. If you can't or won't listen, I'll confiscate your weapons or, better yet, let you try to handle this alone. How long do you think you'll last against several clans of rogue night elves? A day? A week? How long?"

She slammed her sword on the table and planted her feet shoulder width apart, fisting her hands on her hips.

The clan members put away their weapons and scowling, sat in the assorted chairs, grudgingly giving Skye their attention.

"Thank you. I will vouch for Aethel."

He snapped his head up and stared at the warrior gnome.

"I have known this particular night elf longer than most of you have been on this planet. His heart is pure and his intentions honorable. He can no more choose his heritage than your or I but this man...this night elf guarded this valley from outside sources long before your families settled here.

"When my cousin described the invaders of her village, I knew immediately what we were facing. Glade has been true to his word. He and his clansmen are terrorizing the mountains and valley.

"Singularly, we stand no chance of saving our community.

However if we unite, pool our resources and plan wisely, I believe we can defeat these marauders and run them out of our lives forever.

"Who's with me?"

Silence permeated the room. Each clan leader glanced at the other.

"Fine. Then you can kiss your loved ones and dig holes in the ground to be buried because alone we won't make it."

Skye grabbed her blade and headed to the door.

"What about him?"

She spun around to face the speaker. "Who?"

"The traitor night elf."

Skye walked to Aethel and placed her hand on his shoulder, ignoring the spark she felt flame in her heart.

"You call him a traitor; I call him a hero. He could have easily decided to throw his sword in with the mercenaries burning their way through our homes, but chose instead to stand up and be counted with us. His life is in danger every moment of the day because of his choice.

"Can you say the same?"

Low conversations buzzed in the air until Fergus of the river gnomes stood.

"I'll throw my sword in with you. But only if you lead, Skye."

Heads around the room nodded.

Skye stood straight and lifted her chin. "Fine. I'll take the lead on this but there is one hard and fast rule."

"What?"

"Do *not* question my orders or my authority. The first time either is put in doubt, I'll walk away and leave you to your own devices. Are we clear?"

"Aye."

"Form the circle."

The clan heads circled, facing the center, and placed their blade tip on top of the next.

Skye was the last to place her blade on the wheel of steel.

"These blades will fight for heart and home, until this land is again our own."

"To the death!"

Skye put up her free hand. "No. To life!"

"TO LIFE!"

The cry echoed through the building. When the swords had been sheathed and clan leaders filed out, Aethel stood from his seat.

"You took a huge chance today, Skye. Why?"

She gazed into the blue eyes which set her pulse racing. "Because I truly believe you are a man of honor, Aethel. You could have decided to throw your lot with the mercenaries. The one thing I didn't mention in the meeting was my cousin described a she elf with flowing silver hair in white leathers. You and I know there is only one person who fits that description."

"Gitty."

"Yes. But I didn't want these chieftains to have that bit of information. They wouldn't have united. They don't understand children who don't obey their parents. In our culture, it isn't tolerated or understood.

"Will you be able to help us even if it means working against your own kin?"

Aethel moved close to Skye. "Yes. I have love for my children but I don't have to like them. I do, however, wish to protect those I love and like. Will you allow me that honor?"

Skye felt the heat rush to her cheeks. It'd been a long time since any man had brought such personal feelings to the top of her heart. As much as she tried, denying her feelings for Aethel was going to be near impossible. She still loved him as much as ever.

She cleared her throat. "Thank you for helping our community."

Aethel leaned over and picked up her hand, placing a gentle kiss on the top.

"My pleasure."

Skye slipped her hand from his, knowing her cheeks were blazing red.

"Won't you be in danger if you go home?"

"Probably. I'll bunk at the inn until we've secured our valley. What about you? You surely can't go home with Glade and his clan roaming the woods."

"Hhmm. I hadn't thought of that. Well…"

"Allow me to pay for a room for you at the inn, too."

"Aethel..."

He smiled at her dangerous tone. She was always independent and determined to make her own way. It was a trait he admired.

"As you just pointed out to me, the danger out there is real."

Skye huffed out a deep breath. "Fine. But know I'll have the innkeeper marking down the costs so I can repay you."

Aethel smiled. "Of course."

Skye grabbed her sword and sheathed it. "Let's go. I find myself sporting a great hunger. You?"

"Aye. The innkeeper is quite a good cook. The food will fill the belly and please the soul."

Marching out the door and down the dusty road, the unlikely duo headed to the small community of humans. The war had begun.

Chapter Thirteen

Gitty sat in the caravan reveling in the tales Glade was spinning of his conquests of the small towns and villages.

"We galloped in and, blades whirling, took down all the menfolk. As you would expect, some of the women were in gear and fighting back so my kinsmen felt no remorse in taking them down too.

"Ahhh, Gitty, it was a sight. The first hut was set ablaze and the others went up in the blink of an eye. What a vision! I believe we'll be in control of this land in less than six moons. Taking their land is as easy as swirling a finger through water.

"Our deal is still in place, right?"

Gitty stretched her legs under the table and pushed her arms over her head.

"Of course. I just set the paperwork in motion to buy this mountain for you. When the bank manager approves the sale and issues the money to the human, we'll own everything you see.

"Will that keep your kinsmen happy?"

"Yes. Some of them are beginning to grumble a bit. They want a challenge in battle. So far none of these outposts have provided them a contest worthy of their talents."

"Tell them to have a little patience. By the fall of the first leaves, they can start wooing their sweethearts and planning little warriors."

Smiling, she rose from the table. "I've enjoyed the tales of valor, love, but I must go home. Can't have your kinfolk talking, can we?"

Glade blocked her path and snatched her into his arms. He leaned down and pulled her earlobe gently into his mouth. Releasing the soft tissue, he whispered.

"No, can't have the neighbors telling stories out of school."

Gitty moaned and turned her face to his accepting his lips. Fire raged through her body, tingling her skin and taking away her breath. She pushed him away.

"I-I have to go."

She rushed out the door and leapt on her stallion, galloping away from the camp to the sound of laughter chasing her out of the woods.

~ * ~

Dorinda stood in front of the assorted group, feeling her knees threatening to give way. She cleared her throat.

"Thank you all for showing up on such short notice. We don't often get together like this, but what I learned recently made me feel this was something of an emergency."

"What is it, Dorinda? You finally getting hitched?"

A ripple of laughter circled the room. Dorinda couldn't help but smile.

"No, Ollie. There's still no man in my life. You volunteering?"

More laughter.

"Okay, okay. I'm sure some of you have noticed we have had quite a few new folk in our community."

Heads bobbed up and down in agreement.

"Now, normally, as a business woman I wouldn't say that is bad, but what I've noticed is these folks seem to be flashing quite a bit of cash around."

"And that's bad?"

The group snickered.

"No, Dave, it's not unless you start thinking about how many of your neighbors are no longer in this room. Anybody seen the Thompsons lately? How about the Williams or the McCoys? Tell me, who else is missing?"

The gathered group started looking around and murmuring.

Realization started to dawn on the members present.

"Dorinda, what's happening?"

"I made a trip to town to make my final payment on the inn and restaurant and got the bank president to talking. In the last three months, ten folk have sold their places to the family up on the hill--the Sauns. Most of the sales went to the young man, Morgan, but it seems the girl, Gitty, is now starting to purchase land.

"Have any of you been approached?"

Several hands rose in the air.

"Do you see what's happening here? If we don't watch out, they'll own every bit of land around here and all our hard work will be for nothing. To be honest with you, I don't think I want to live here if they become the main landowners.

"I've watched that young man when he comes in the pub. It makes my skin crawl just to think about it. If that doesn't scare you, think about this...Morgan Saun had no problem running a sword through a stranger who insulted his lady. What would he do to someone who hunted on his land or tried to plant wheat in his valley?

""We need to hang on to our property. If they're bound and determined to buy it, make them wait. What's the big hurry?"

"Okay. I've said my piece. Who wants lunch?"

Dorinda watched as the members of her community bunched in small groups. She might not be able to completely stop the sale of her valley, but the Sauns weren't going to walk in and take over. Not if she had anything to say about it.

~ * ~

Tiamoon moved her feet slowly and watched every movement she made. Whispers had the night elves planning a raid on this settlement tonight. She, Terran and a dozen of her family clan had volunteered to patrol the perimeter of the village.

The shadows at the edge of the meadow stretched long into the forest backdrop. Every movement set Tia's teeth on edge. Her muscles ached from the intense control and her hands itched to be fighting.

"Tia." The whisper reverberated off the pines.

"What?" She couldn't stop the irritation in her voice. Of all people, Terran should know better than to try and communicate when they were on silent watch.

"I need to answer the call of nature."

"Now?"

"Yes."

"Then be as quiet as you can."

Muffled steps crushed against the needle strewn forest floor. Tia's ears keened to hear any unusual movements.

"AAAAHHHHH!!!!"

"TERRAN!"

The sound of her brother's cry set Tia racing in the direction she recalled him going.

"TERRAN!"

Thundering hoof beats came toward her. In her quick estimate, she guessed a dozen horses were heading her direction.

"INTRUDERS! INTRUDERS!"

She clutched her sword to her chest and nitched against a large pine. As the hoof beats rumbled closer, she muttered. "Please forgive me."

Turning the blade side away from the animal's shin, she grabbed the blade and swung the handle side at the animal with all her might.

The horse stumbled, sending the rider to the ground. Behind him two others went down. Tia rushed out and finished the night elf with a swift blow. She quickly glanced at the figure on the ground and caught her breath. She'd just put a sword through Glade. The ashen color of his skin indicated her prowess had not lessened since the last war.

Not having the time to think further on the situation, Tiamoon soon dispatched two other elven warriors. She ran between the trees to the village. Slowing her pace to a trot, she noted smoke rising from the chimneys and lights in the windows. She spun to face the remaining warriors headed this direction but heard no hoof beats echoing through the pines.

Tiamoon slowed her breathing and narrowed her eyes. A movement in the trees set her teeth to grinding as she tensed to fight. Three forms headed her direction. Two upright figures dragged a limp form between them. Tia's muscles went into overdrive.

She moved silently toward the trio.

"Tia?" A whisper pierced her concentration.

"Frey?"

"Yes. We've Terran and he's hurt bad. We need to get him to the healer."

She ran to the cottage known to house the healer and knocked on the door.

A sliver of light cut the darkness of the night as the gnome witch peeked out the door.

"What is it you need?"

"My brother is badly wounded. We need your healing powers."

"Bring him to me."

Tia ran to relieve one of the warriors. Moving with urgency, the gnomes made their way to the healer's cottage. Directed to a cot by the fire, Terran was laid on the straw mattress.

The healer turned to the warriors, centering her gaze on Tiamoon.

"Go. I will send for you when I have ministered to him."

"But..."

"Go. Your bond to him is too strong. It will interfere with my healing efforts."

Tia glared at the healer but left the cottage. She was a warrior, not a healer, and could respect the witch's need to perform her magic in private.

When the sun rose above the eastern mountains, a small child came and tugged on the tail of Tia's cloak.

"You must come to the healer's."

She hurried to follow the child and knocked before entering the cottage of the witch.

The woman looked up. "I'm truly sorry but they damaged his life source. I could do nothing to save him."

Tia looked at the broken form of her brother. She clenched her jaw, spun on her heel and left the healer's cottage. Barging past the gathered warriors, she barked orders.

"Give Terran a warrior's burial then head to your homes. The night has been long and we need rest before the next attack."

The men glanced warily at each other. Many had fought with her in the last war and knew this look did not bode well for the enemy. Many night elves would lose their lives to pay for the death of Tiamoon's brother.

Chapter Fourteen

Morgan paced the living room end to end. His deal on the Huff land had fallen through and for no reason he could fathom. He'd offered them more money than they could hope to get in a lifetime, yet just as they were about to agree to his terms, they changed their mind. The same situation occurred with the Millers down by the stream. If he didn't know better, he'd swear someone was undermining him. *Gitty?*

Scuffing across the floor in house boots on her feet, she meandered through to the kitchen, an enigmatic smile on her face. She hummed a Celtic tune she recalled her mother singing years earlier.

"What are you so happy about?" Morgan scowled at her.

"Why not? From what I hear, the forest elves are ridding the surrounding mountains of all the worthless creatures usurping our land."

Morgan stared at his sister. "What did you just say?"

Gitty rolled her eyes. "The forest elves are ridding the mountains of all the scum. Dragons, Morgan, don't you ever read?"

"Why? Won't make me rich."

"Seems you're not getting that way by your own means. Maybe reading will help you become the noble landowner you think you should be." She smirked his direction.

"I knew it! *You're* the one who's undermining my deals." He shot toward her, fury overcoming common sense.

Before Morgan could reach Gitty, she'd pulled a knife and held it at his throat, the blade inches from his Adam's apple.

"Don't tempt me, little brother. I've always wanted to be an only child. If your deals aren't working out, it's not because I'm undermining them. It's because you're a poor negotiator. I'm not experiencing problems."

He backed away and shot her a dirty look.

"If father were here, he'd tell you to back off. As the heir apparent, it's your duty to support me and my efforts."

Gitty's brows furrowed as she stared at her brother. She broke into laughter and walked away. "But he isn't here, is he? In fact, I haven't seen him in several weeks, Morgan. Have you?"

Morgan gazed out the window and mulled over Gitty's statement. She was right. He hadn't seen his father in several weeks. He walked back to the master bedroom and entered. The bed was properly made and a light layer of dust covered the furniture tops. Opening the wardrobe, Morgan noted Aethel's riding boots were missing and his leathers appeared to be gone. He quick-stepped his way to the stables. Several fighting blades used by Aethel were missing, as was the thoroughbred mare he always rode.

If Aethel was gone then...he liked the idea of being the head of the house.

Gitty passed him on her way to the barns.

"Don't get any wild ideas about being the boss."

He whipped around. "What?"

"You had that dreamy look on your face like when you think you're going to get your way. Father is still in the area, just not here right now. I've seen him come in, change his clothing and leave. He usually checks to see if either of us is here.

"I believe, little brother, he fears us. If your buying deals are falling apart, our own father maybe responsible. What will you do if he's the one spoiling your plans? Kill him?"

Morgan growled. "I wouldn't be the first or the last to commit patricide, I suspect. I need to regroup. Where are you going?"

Gitty flipped her hair over her shoulder. "None of your business. Don't wait up. I'll be home late." She trotted through the stable opening, reappearing on her steed, and galloped down the driveway.

Morgan fumed as he stomped into the house, slamming the door in his wake.He could sense Gitty was scheming against him and now he had to contend with his father conspiring against him, too? *What to do? What to do?*

"Well, pacing the floor here won't get things done. Maybe there's a young maiden new to the valley who'll appreciate my attentions. A bit of mead will help clear the brain and set the mind to working. That's what I'll do...go to the pub."

Grasping his night cloak, Morgan swung the cape about his shoulders and headed to the barn. He'd find a solution to his situation at the pub and things would go his way in the morning...just like always.

~ * ~

Gnomes, leprechauns and clans of fair night elves tromped in and out of the inn. Dorinda hadn't seen this much business in her family's restaurant, well, ever. During the evening hours, magical folk she'd grown up hearing the tales of came in for food and meetings. Her back rooms were beginning to resemble war rooms. Maps were constantly being unfolded and lines followed by fingers. Murmured conversations soon overtook the music from the radio. When she entered the room with beverages, the dialogues would cease until she left. No matter. Dorinda was thrilled to know the valley where she resided was guarded by the magic folk.

She started leaving plates out on the hearth at night and at the back door. Let the people talk. She knew she was ensuring her safety.

During the day, the farmers and villagers began to stop by and keep her posted on the offers being made by the tall blonde female and male newcomers. Offers met with negative answers.

But of all the wonders in her world, Dorinda was most fascinated by the unusual couple residing in her inn. She tried not to stare, but they brought looks to themselves from everyone.

It had been a month since she'd held the meeting with the village folk and the tall gent and tiny lady in leather clothing sat at a table in her restaurant speaking in low tones. Dorinda watched them, a spike of envy touching her heart. The pair were obviously in love, but something about their conversation suggested they held the worries of the world on their shoulders.

She came over to fill their water glasses.

"Excuse me, miss?" The gentleman's blue eyes held her attention.

"Dorinda, sir. How can I help you?"

He glanced at his companion and she nodded her head.

"You believe in the wee folk, don't you?"

"Yes. My mum was from the old country."

His smile sparkled lighting up his face. "Good. Could you spare my companion and me some time after you close tonight?"

"Sure. I can meet you in the sitting room around 10:00 pm if you wish."

"Perfect."

Dorinda watched as the two held hands. Her curiosity was wildly peaked. If she could only make it until ten without exploding...

~ * ~

Gitty tore through the forest. She hadn't heard from Glade in several days. He always sent a messenger bird after a successful battle and she hadn't heard a thing. Her stomach ached with worry. Slowing her steed, she pulled him to a stop and dismounted. She tied him to the nearest tree opting to walk the rest of the way to the caravan camp.

She followed the trail she'd memorized, breathing easier as the forest opened to the clearing. But the scene unfolding before her struck fear in her heart. The fire pit was black and dark. There were no caravans to be seen anywhere and by the disturbed dirt on the forest floor; the inhabitants had left in a hurry. Gitty ran to the spot where Glade's caravan had stood. Jammed into the ground through his green jerkin was his bloodied sword. Next to the sword stood his riding boots covered in blood.

Gitty sucked air into her lungs. Dropping to her knees, her fingers trembled as she reached out to the boots.

"No." The word whooshed from her mouth.

Snapping twigs alerted her to the presence of another. She looked up to see a haggard-faced, young forest night elf.

"Twelve went out, one came back. Keep your mountain and your wretched valley. It's not worth the price. He loved you more than any other woman and would have presented you many healthy sons. You wasted his life."

The young warrior spit on the ground next to her, turned on his heel and disappeared into the towering pines.

Gitty sat on her heels, determined to be strong, but the moment her hand touched the soft, green leather jerkin, she broke down and wept, the sighing wind through the pine boughs harmonizing with her keening wails.

It was at that moment any compassion felt by the she night elf disappeared.

Chapter Fifteen

Cary and Conn hid beneath the oak their wings shaking in fear.

"So you want to stay? For what? To spend the rest of your life hiding in a tree?"

Dozens of footfalls trampled past the oak and down the road.

Conn buzzed to the center of the room. "I'm not afraid. I just didn't want them to find you."

Cary narrowed her eyes at him. "You're a fool and a liar. What I wouldn't give to find that big red thing that dropped us here and fly away home."

Conn crossed his arms and lifted his head. "I'm not a liar. I'm not afraid."

The ground next to their tree rumbled and rocked the roots of the tree.

Cary screamed and flew to Conn's arms. "What is it? Are we going to die?"

Conn shook her from him and winged his way to the tree's opening. He peeked out the door. Turning, he flashed Cary a huge smile.

"Your magic seems to work just as well here as it did back home."

She furrowed her brows. "What are you talking about? I haven't cast a spell in many moons."

He wiggled his brows. "That big red thing is outside the door and the mangy mutt is running around sniffing. You ready to leave?"

Before he could blink his eyes, Cary had zipped past him and found the opening in the red thing. Recalling the thunderous, rowdy crowd of warriors who'd just passed by, Conn was a wing beat behind her.

He'd had enough adventure for one lifetime.

~ * ~

Morgan swaggered into the pub and reconnoitered the room. There were no night elves, no gnomes, no magic folk at all in the inn. The only woman at the bar was a grandmotherly type drinking cola.

He sauntered to the bar, removed his cloak and sat on a stool. Dorinda appeared and walked toward him.

"He's not welcome here, innkeeper."

The deep voice boomed through the empty room.

Morgan swiveled his chair to look upon a familiar face.

"Father. Since when do you give orders in this place?" A sneer marred the young night elf's chiseled features.

"Since the council gave me the power over all things in the valley and mountains. We've watched you try and steal what these humans have worked so hard to earn by playing to their sense of security. No longer, Morgan. You are not welcome on these premises. Your presence is offensive to all creatures magical and nonmagical.

"When you took the life of an Other without regard..."

"But *he* offended my companion and *he* is the one who issued the challenge." Morgan smirked, his knowledge of the rules of dueling well honed.

"Truth that may well be, but you could also tell from his ways and clothing he was not of this time."

Morgan shrugged. "I can't help it if he didn't know where he was."

"And that attitude is what has gotten you banned. Until this generation has grandchildren or has passed on, you will confine yourself to the castle grounds starting now."

Standing with his hand on his blade, the young night elf glared at his father.

"Are you going to enforce this decision?"

Aethel stood tall. "If you force me, I'll do whatever it takes to obey the council's decree. Don't push me, Morgan. I *will* cross swords with you and I'll win."

The air crackled with electricity and the two night elves faced each other. Morgan dropped his hand from his sword.

"This is a poor excuse for a proper pub anyway. I'll find my entertainment elsewhere." He snatched his cloak and stormed from the room.

Dorinda watched the older night elf melt away from the room. She looked up to see if Betty needed another cola only to find the seat empty. As the time was nearing ten, she locked the front door and started to clean up.

At the appointed time, Dorinda joined Skye and Aethel in the dining room. The three sat at a table staring at each other.

"What is it you wish to talk to me about?" Dorinda's voice wavered.

Skye smiled and gently touched her hand. "Don't be afraid. We're not here to harm anyone. We've watched you with the Others. You sense things they don't and I suspect you have the magic about you."

Dorinda felt the heat rush to her cheeks. How could this small woman see so well?

"Uhm, yes. It's strong in my family. My grandmother was a healer back in Ireland before we came here. I've been taught the old ways since I was a child."

"Aha! I knew I'd been feeling old magic in the air." Aethel rose from the chair and began to pace. "Are there many other humans with this power?"

Dorinda shook her head. "No. I'm afraid once I'm gone the old magic will die. No one in this country believes as I do and I don't believe they want to. They're too busy trying to survive in the here and now."

Aethel stopped pacing and stood behind Skye. "We asked you here to be an ambassador for the Others until the uprising has been quelled."

Dorinda sat back in her chair. *Me? An ambassador?*

Skye reached a hand out and touched the innkeeper's lightly. "You know that Aethel and his kin are night elves, right?"

"I guessed."

"I'm a gnome. While originally of the forest clan, I moved to the meadow and joined them when I wed. There are also wood nymphs, leprechauns and wee folk in the surrounding areas. We need an advocate who can make the Others, the humans, understand our plight. I know most humans in this country don't believe in us but they seem to listen to you.

"Will you speak for us?"

Sucking air into her lungs, Dorinda's only answer was a large smile.

Aethel patted Skye gently on the back. "I told you she would."

Skye rolled her eyes and huffed. "Men."

Aethel turned his attention to Dorinda. "The worst of the uprising has passed but there might be pockets of resistance to the peace plan we've set in place. We need you and your kind to be wary and let us know when unusual happenings occur. We'll send out our warriors to keep control of the few. I promise no human will be harmed."

Dorinda looked to the earnest faces of her guests. "How can I say no?"

"Then it is done." Aethel patted Skye's shoulder.

"It's done." Skye nodded her agreement.

"It's done." Dorinda agreed.

~ * ~

Tiamoon stood at the cottage's door gazing on the carefully manicured yard. When Skye had learned of Terran's death, she'd come back and worked furiously in the yard for three days, digging until her fingers bled. Tia knew her mother had watered the plants with her tears.

But Tia had been surprised when Skye had gone back to the inn, especially when Skye sent word via the mouse network she'd be staying with Aethel, the night elf.

Skye had instructed Tiamoon to retrieve a diary she kept in her wardrobe. The contents would explain her actions.

As instructed by her mother, Tia had read the early pages and received the shock of her life. She was half night elf. She wasn't sure whether to scorn herself or deny the connection. What she did was send a message to her mother to find her happiness.

Maybe among all the death there would be a spark of love and a promise of life. Only time would tell.

Discover the rest of the story in
A St. Patrick's Day Tale
by
Christine Young, C. L. Kraemer, Genene Valleau

Tumble through time…

…to Ireland in 1817, when tensions are high between Protestants and Catholics and fae people guide the fate of villagers. A lovely Catholic lass stumbles upon the weakly ritual fisticuffing between Irish lads. She falls into the lap of a handsome young Protestant. Family ties, grudges, and two conniving faeries threaten their budding love. But the faeries outsmart themselves when they hijack a time machine that has mysteriously appeared in their forest and are whisked to…

…Eugene, Oregon in the 20th century, amid a property feud between the local faeries and night elves. The conniving faeries from Olde Ireland try to stir up more mischief. However, a warrior gnome convinces the magic folk to control their own destiny, and forces the intruding faeries to take refuge in the time machine again, spinning their way toward…

…A modern day castle in western Oregon. An eccentric inventor is determined to reclaim his wayward time machine and save his beloved wife from her latest misadventure. If only they can travel safely past the black hole…

Available at Rogue Phoenix Press
www.roguephoenixpress.com

Other books by Christie L. Kraemer
Available at Rogue Phoenix Press

Healthy Homicide

Two murders have occurred at the Barrel Springs Day Spa. Police hurry to find the method and reason before anyone else is murdered.

MANIC READER REVIEWS says: Healthy Homicide by C.L. Kraemer is an intriguing plot driven mystery. The plot is well written and pretty much carries the whole story...

Dragons Among Us

In a world full of anomalies such as the platypus and self reproducing Komodo dragon, is the human race willing to accept that dragons may be real?

Sapien Draconi-human-dragon shape shifters-all over the world face this dilemma every day. The question has become life and death as their species is plagued with unexpected and unwanted shifting in the most unlikely of places.

The Ancient Ones-full-blooded dragons-can offer advice, but few seem to put forward workable solutions to the problem.

The fate of the shape shifters hangs in the balance, and an answer must be found before the Homo Sapiens find, dissect, and hunt Sapien Draconi to extinction.

Dragons Among The Eagles

Aleda Sable faces the toughest decision of her life--to stay in dragon form, live as a two-legged or put one foot in the human world and one talon in the dragon world.

An urgent call from her newspaper editor sends Aleda to report on an accident whose driver appears to be a dragon. Authorities have the scene locked down and aren't allowing access to anyone. Television broadcasts flash pictures of scaly legs hanging from a crashed car. However, the bodies disappear into thin air. When the stations try follow-up reports, all they find are state highway workers busily tearing up the roads.

In determining the truth of the shifter disappearances, Aleda finds the truth of her own dilemma.

Shattered Tomorrows

Lucy Daniels has a secret--a deeply guarded secret.

Her life was going along just fine until she accompanied her best friend, Cassie, to her attorney's suite on top of the Equitable Building in downtown Salem, Oregon.

Once inside the lawyer's office, the world turned upside down and Lucy was forced to face a demon from her past. Thirty years ago, life had been different. Lucy had discovered Prince Charming and was headed to her happily ever after.

That's when the devil intervened and because of her brush with the devil, innocent people died.

C. L. Kraemer
is also featured in these anthologies available at
Rogue Phoenix Press

A Different Kind of Valentine

A collection of four short stories:

Witness by k. J. Dahlen

When Colten finds an injured woman the police are looking for her, should he trust his own judgement about keeping her hidden from the law even if it means she might kill him?

The Prize by C. L. Kraemer

A computer geek learns valuable life lessons when he is given his dream car as well as a condo and the perfect job.

Crazy 'bout You by Clay Renick

Can a psychologist and a romance writer find true love in time for Valentines Day?

Time Changes by Nicolette Zamora

Laurie is just about ready to give up on love when she spies Rob Hender, her high school sweethearts older brother.

A Valentine's Anthology

The Lending Library-a fantasy by C. L. Kraemer

Faeries try to fit into the human world when the forest where they make their home is destroyed by a mysterious enemy.

Chasing Rainbows-a contemporary romance by Genene Valleau

An eccentric aunt, an inventive uncle, a mother who wears poodle skirts, and a brother who wears pearls provide a hilarious backdrop for the courtship of a young woman who yearns for a "normal" family.

The Gift-an historical romance by Christine Young

A man and a woman on opposite sides of the Civil War get a second chance at love after one final battle returns soldiers to their war-torn homes to rebuild their lives.